SEX CHANGE:

(A Nina Bannister Mystery)

by

T'Gracie and Joe Reese

For information, email **Cozy Cat Press**, cozycatpress@aol.com or visit our website at: www.cozycatpress.com

COZY CAT
P R E S S

ISBN: 978-1-939816-51-1

Printed in the United States of America

Cover design by Kari Klawiter
http://artbykarri.com/cover-art

1 2 3 4 5 6 7 8 9 10

"Men are men; but Man is a woman."
—Chesterton

Dedicated to the women in the
United States House of Representatives

PROLOGUE: PORPHYRIA'S LOVER

It was his first night in the new apartment.

Apartment?

It was hardly an apartment; it was a hovel. They had rented it to him as a "garden apartment," but of course there was no garden. There was only the sidewalk just beyond the window. He had to keep the window open, for otherwise there would have been no air at all; but this meant he could hear the sound of feet scuffling by on the sidewalk.

Scuffling.

A good word.

It was what rats did. And he was now little more than a rat.

He had once been a "literary man;" for that matter, he had once been a "man."

Those days were over now, of course, because of the dreadful thing he had done.

But literature remained in his brain to taunt him.

"I am a spiteful man. I am a little man. I think my liver is diseased."

The Underground Man.

And here he now found himself, underground.

Pipes bellowed around him when water from the tenements above coursed through them.

And otherwise...

...otherwise there was nothing to listen to, nothing to brighten the shadows, or make the two or three pieces of shabby and worn furniture more comforting.

This, this was what he had come to.

He continued to sit on the bed for a time, looking out of the window, watching the shoes rasp by.

Then he picked up the one book he had brought with him from his other life.

The page he needed was marked, and so he simply let the book fall open.

There was a candle burning on the desk by the bed, so he had just enough light to read.

Browning.

The poem was "Porphyria's Lover," in which a man of lower caste, jilted by his aristocratic lover, "searches for a thing to do," when receiving her for a final visit. He then says:

> "I found
> A thing to do, and all her hair
> In one long yellow string I wound
> Three times her little throat around,
> And strangled her.
> I propp'd her head up as before...
> And all night long we have not stirr'd,
> And yet God has not said a word!"

He read the poem several times, holding it close to the flickering orange flame, watching the smoke drift out through the window.

Then he took a knife from the drawer of the desk, carefully cut out the page on which the work appeared, and held the page in the candle flame until it blackened.

He let the charred ashes fall into a wastebasket at his feet.

He glanced at the luminous dial of a clock sitting in front of him.

Two o'clock in the morning.

And still people came and went outside, most of them leaving the bars scattered along the street, most of them, almost certainly, drunk.

He lay down on the bed and stared at the ceiling, waiting for God to speak to him.

For he was not like the murderer in Browning's poem.

God *would* speak to him.

God *had* spoken to him!

Then he became aware of the voice within him, calling him.

Unfortunately, it was not God.

CHAPTER 1: MANGER SCENE

The atmosphere in the town hall was electric. It was the same central meeting chamber it had always been—gray desks pockmarked with the small curved designs made by nervous fingernails on a malleable surface—and it had neither grown in dimensions nor increased in dramatic potential.

No, it was simply a town hall.

Bigger and more modern than some, perhaps, because Bay St. Lucy had spent a part of its recent influx in funds in building it from scratch, based on the most modern of designs.

But there was very little anyone could do when designing a civic building.

It was a place where boring things had to be done, by people who were bored doing them.

And yet this night was different.

TV monitors had been put up on walls where none had been the day before.

Coffee patrols had been organized, and small brown cups kept moving up and down lines of people like water in bucket brigades.

And as for the people, they spoke in hushed tones.

As did Nina Bannister.

"When was the last report?" she was asking.

Coffee moving by, coffee moving by...

"Eight thirty five," came the answer, from any one of four or five distracted and haggard citizens who might have given it.

"Look! New report coming!"

All six of the large TV screens that encircled the room went dark simultaneously, then relit anew, in order to show an attractive blonde woman standing in front of the Mississippi State House.

"Hello; I'm Glenda Barker reporting from Jackson. Polls have been closed now across the state for a little over two hours, and we're getting some ideas now about the way this special election is shaping up."

"How are you doing, Nina?"

Macy Cox.

"I'm all right, Macy. I'm just ready for it to be over, one way or another."

"I understand. We all do."

"May I have your attention, please!"

No one had noticed that the door at the room's main entrance had opened.

But it had.

No one had noticed that Edie Towler had walked into it.

But she had.

No one had noticed that she now held before her a clip board much like the one Macy was carrying around.

But she did.

And now, with that quiet confidence and understated authority that Edie always seemed to exude, she was speaking:

"You don't have to listen to the broadcast going on up there. That's just NBC going over things you already know. We know something, though, that they don't. It just came in here; they won't get it for a few minutes. We always get updates first. So I can tell you this now."

The room fell silent.

Almost.

There was the whirring of ventilation systems in the ceiling, the scuffle of feet as people positioned themselves so as to get a better look at Edie, the rattle rattle slurp slurp of the entire coffee apparatus now in operation, its Styrofoam and balsa wood rattle-patter and ever present background noise.

Other than that, though, silence, as Edie said:

"Rankin, Jefferson, and Peterson Counties. Now too close to call."

The room caught its breath.

They were all there, all the denizens of Bay St. Lucy.

Alanna Delafosse, seated beneath the window, a street light shining through the half-closed blinds and making her face a caramel glow; John Giusti talking on a cell phone, nodding, whispering, imploring somebody to do something and do it fast, because this was it, and time was dwindling; John's wife Helen, late of the Broadway stage, seated a few feet away from her husband, her face fixed on a computer screen; Jackson Bennett, all six feet three of him, immaculately gray-suited, standing still as a statue, only his lips moving as he totaled figures known to no one but himself, and visualized consequences and concerns which, Nina knew as the widow of a lawyer, were only visible to those who knew *The Law* in its capital letter sense.

Even Tom Broussard, who did nothing civil, who was not civil—even Tom was seated in a far corner rattling on a computer keyboard, either writing press releases or grisly murder stories.

And there, bringing him a cup of something, ostensibly coffee, more probably bourbon or some unknown brew even stronger, was his wife of not quite a year—Penelope Royale.

Penelope was now four months pregnant.

But tonight she was working like everyone else.

Worrying like everyone else.

Nina tried to make sense of what Edie had just said.

Rankin, Jefferson, and Peterson Counties.

Too close to call.

Incredible.

It led her back to a scene in February.

When in February, the first week?

Yes, of course, because that was, and had been for ages, the week of the Swordfish Jubilee, held in Bay St. Lucy in the middle of winter, when the weather was too cold in most other states to have a fair or any other type of outdoor celebration.

The Jubilee featured amazing opportunities for deep sea fishing.

But it also featured the closest thing the city had to a county fair, with midway, rides, and everything else.

One of the best county fairs in the state of Mississippi, everybody said so.

Nina loved it, and had always loved it, from the days in childhood when she rode the wildest rides again and again and again and tried to knock the weighted bottles off their little three-legged stools and failed, of course, but kept trying because the tickets were only fifty cents for five throws and there were, high on a shelf above the bottles themselves, THOSE MARVELOUS STUFFED ANIMALS!

Now she went for the food.

But what food!

Booth after booth: Fletchers' Original Corny Dogs, Sam Jackson's Funnel Cakes, Hot Dogs Galore!, Italian Ice Treats, Fried Onion Rings, Bratwurst, Southern Fried Chicken, Pizza by the Slice—and of course, for Bay St. Lucy was a fishing village—fish fish fish of all kinds, fried or broiled or blackened or whole or half or in parts or in little bits or still live, swimming around in the tank, for you to knock on the head and take home and do with as you pleased.

Octopus.

Fried octopus rings!

...and on and on.

There was wrestling, judging, guitar playing, craft booths, photography booths, weight guessing, kiss buying,...

...all of these things as usual.

This year had been different, though.

Something else had happened.

She had arrived at ten o'clock in the morning, the way she always did; had paid her three dollar admission fee (but gotten her wrist stamped so she could come back in); had eaten herself silly and slightly sick; had Vespa'd home to Furl and bed; had napped the afternoon away; had revitalized herself around sundown and then returned to a much different setting, all glowing in the dark now, every midway attraction a bit louder and more garish, the whole fair shimmering in the twilight, vaguely wicked, its morning smile having turned, with the surrounding darkness, into something more like a leer.

This did not matter to her in the least. The only thing that mattered was that she had become, thank heaven, once again hungry, and could make the rounds of all the booths again.

She had done about half of this and was wandering aimlessly by the 'judging' buildings, making a horrid mess of a blooming onion, most of which had bloomed down onto her sweatshirt and some of which had gotten, impossibly, into her hair, when a barker stepped out of the rabbit exhibition and beckoned to her:

"Hey, Miss! Yeah, you! C'mere!"

The barker smiled, stepped forward, repeated himself, grinned, and finally was transformed by the light of a nearby Ferris Wheel into Jackson Bennett.

Jackson was the biggest thing at the fair, and, though not the most intimidating, still ranked pretty high on the scary list, and could still have frightened silly the same linebackers he had run over a couple of decades ago while playing ball at LSU.

"Yeah, you! Yeah, you!"

"Jackson!"

Nina smiled and allowed herself to be taken in by whatever shell game was about to be played.

Because, whatever it was going to be, Jackson always seemed to be there at the start of it.

And now, here he was again, inviting her into a rabbit barn.

A rabbit barn.

What could that lead to?

But she greeted him, shook his mammoth hand with her puppet-like one (she always felt like a puppet in his presence), and allowed herself to be led farther into the building.

Soon there were hutches of rabbits on either side of her.

Brown rabbits, black rabbits, reddish rabbits, and white rabbits.

She felt like Alice in Wonderland.

And so on they went, talking of this and that, how wonderful it all was, had she eaten enough, was she planning to stay until it closed, what did she think of the smells here in the livestock barns, and, yes, livestock were livestock weren't they and wasn't it warm on the midway this year especially for February and there was indeed some talk of rain, even tonight, but, no, everyone knew it didn't rain at night in February in Mississippi and now there were sheep beside them instead of rabbits and now there were goats and the long, long structure continued to stretch before them until...

...until—there—sitting on a couple of hay bales, straw beside them, 4-H members hopping over them and avoiding them if possible...

...was a group plotting some outrage.

It just had that feel to it.

Alanna Delafosse.

How in God's name had anyone gotten Alanna Delafosse into a livestock barn?

But there she was, Fifth Avenue Alanna, decked out for *Vogue* magazine in a huge-brimmed black straw hat and a white dress with red stars that somehow had remained white when nothing else within half a mile of it was, except buckets and buckets and buckets of milk.

Edie Towler.

Town District Attorney and soul of importance and common sense.

Edie's outfit blended into the straw around it, as her outfits always seemed to blend into the earth, and the natural order of things.

John Giusti.

John, who was the town veterinarian, and the only person in the group who seemed to belong in a livestock barn.

Its only true scientist, and its most brilliant high school graduate ever.

These people.

Along with Macy Cox.

And, finally, sitting on a bale of hay, legs crossed, eyes fixed on Jackson, Paul Cox.

Paul and Macy, one and one half years wed now, still blissful.

Paul, the best high school principal in Bay St. Lucy's history.

Except for Nina.

To whom Jackson Bennett now addressed his remarks.

Thus drawing her into the conspiracy.

"Nina, Jarrod Thornbloom is dead."

"That's terrible. How did it happen?"

"Plane crash. He and a pilot took off in his private plane from D.C., heading to Paris for some international conference. The plane disappeared from the radar screen around noon. The Coast Guard confirmed wreckage an hour later. No survivors."

It could have been a manger scene, with the five of them spread out like wise men and shepherds; the blue jacketed 4Hers running here and there with brushes and buckets; and the dim lights humming high overhead, drawing upward the most agile of flies, those light enough to soar upward and leave their heavier counterparts, like buzzing drops of tar, to bumble about down below.

"Jarrod Thornbloom," said Alanna to the group, "was an institution."

No, Nina found herself thinking. *He should have been in an institution.* And he should not ever have run for the House of Representatives fifteen months earlier.

At eighty one years old he had clearly begun to lose his mental capacity.

Some of his speeches...

But, she mused, he was a venerable fixture in Washington, a revered white-haired man, and he had, through the decades, served the state well.

Now he was gone.

All she could say was:

"I'm sorry. He was a good man."

Silence for a time.

And then Macy, barely able to contain herself:

"Nina, there has to be a special election to replace him until next November."

Jackson:

"The election will be in March. In some states, when a senator or representative cannot finish a term, the governor simply appoints a replacement. But in Mississippi, there has to be an election."

"All right," she said, nodding and wondering what all of this had to do with her.

John Giusti:

"Nina, there is a chance that Paul could run in this election. And that he could win."

Macy beamed at her husband.

Then she said:

"It will be wide open. There will be several candidates. And the chances of a Democrat winning in District 58 this fall are not great. The Republicans have a lot of support."

Jackson interjected:

"But Thornbloom *was* a Democrat, and he somehow managed to get elected time and again, for all these years."

Paul leaned forward:

"Nina, as I've told you a few times, the governor and I have been working well together these last months. We see things the same way. I'm happy to have had the chance to go up to Jackson."

"I know you've done well up there, Paul. We're all proud of you. If anybody has a political career in front of him, it's you."

"I don't know. I do know that the governor called me into his office this afternoon, just after the news broke..."

And now Macy could no longer contain herself:

"He said Paul should run!"

Paul, embarrassed, shook his head:

"Now wait, Macy..."

"But he did, Paul, he did!"

"No. He said perhaps I should *think* about running."

"Isn't that the same thing?"

Smiles around the circle.

Finally Jackson said:

"There are a good many reasons, Paul, to think you might have a shot at this. First, your relationship with the governor certainly won't hurt. Both of you have similar ideas on educational reform. Second, you have Bay St. Lucy, and Bay St. Lucy is rich."

"Are we allowed, as a city, to support a candidate?" asked Nina.

"Of course we are!" answered Jackson. "If the Bay St. Lucy City Council says unanimously—and it will be unanimous—that we want to give a great deal of money to a candidate, because that candidate will advance the interests of our community—why there is no power in the state that could or would stop us."

John Giusti:

"You're a great public speaker, Paul. You were a great athlete, and that's gold in Mississippi. You're young. You've made no political enemies. There are people who disagree with your stance on standardized testing, of course, but…"

Paul shook his head:

"I'm not sure that would be a major consideration. I think, as an ex-principal, I can be certain of the support of all state teachers' organizations. The question is, will that be enough?"

Pause.

"…and the answer is *no*. No, it won't. I'm going to need vocal backing, and financial backing, from several other major powers. And Nina, that's where you come in."

Nina, somewhat taken aback, could only look around the strange circle of people who had gathered in this manger-like setting.

"What?" she found herself stammering.

"I said I need the support of other major powers."

"And I'm a major power?"

"No, but you have close contacts with one."

"What major power do I have contacts with? The Mississippi Cat Owners Association?"

Smiles at this.

Paul:

"No. You have contacts with Gulf Coast Petroleum. They're a billion dollar industry. One of the largest in the state, bigger even than any timber or agricultural organization."

She was beginning to understand.

"Well. I did make some friends there."

"You saved the huge oil rig Aquatica. And in so doing, you saved their reputation, a hundred and fifty three of their employees—and maybe the whole eco-system of the gulf coast."

Jackson Bennett leaned forward:

"Nina, I took the liberty of doing something this afternoon that—well, maybe I shouldn't have."

She looked at him, thinking almost instinctively:

Uh-oh.

Here it comes again.

I'm going to get wrapped up in some incomprehensible and dangerous mess.

On the other hand...

...what kind of a mess could this be?

One of my best friends has a great opportunity.

Why not help him?

If I can.

And so, to Jackson:

"What did you do, Jackson? And what do you want me to do?"

"I called a friend of mine who's one of Gulf Coast Petroleum's attorneys. He's based in Lafayette."

"As is," she said, "the whole oil industry."

"That's right. Anyway, I asked him if there was a possibility that you might fly over there and speak to someone higher up, on Paul's account. Mainly to beg for their support."

"And?"

"You have an appointment tomorrow afternoon with the CEO of Gulf Coast Petroleum, in their downtown offices. I've arranged for your air ticket."

And so, there it was. Nina Bannister was going to Lafayette.

The 'meeting in the livestock barn,' as she now remembered it, had happened months ago, in February.

Now it was Tuesday, March 15, night of the special election to replace Jarrod Thornbloom.

Ten forty-five p.m.

Nina, having just gotten off the phone with some newspaper or other, went outside.

A group of smokers had gathered outside city hall.

Margot Gavin had joined them, after having worked late in her shop, Elementals: Treasures from Earth and Sea. Helen Reddington, not having successfully given up cigarettes, was in the small circle. So was Tom Broussard, slovenly, hulking.

The March sky was also slovenly and hulking, and a cool wind was whistling in from the gulf.

A few cars prowled the street of Bay St. Lucy, which had not quite gotten itself ready for spring break.

Tom made a comment about the weather.

Everybody nodded.

Somebody asked about his latest book.

He answered something or other, forgetting for the moment that he never talked about his books, for the simple reason that no one really cared and had only asked for the simple reason that there was not much else you could talk about with Tom Broussard.

Finally, Helen flipped the stub of whatever she was smoking into the gutter that stretched placidly a few feet from where she stood and asked:

"So how far down are we?"

That was in fact the question Nina had just been answering to the *Biloxi Town Journal*, and so she could say:

"Three hundred and forty seven votes, as of two minutes ago."

"What's left to report?" rumbled Tom.

"Seven counties, all in the north. Desoto, Tippah, Alcorn, Tate, Marshall, Benton, Prentiss."

Margot huddled more tightly inside her Chicago Bears windbreaker and asked:

"They're rural, aren't they?"

Nina could not help smiling.

"All of Mississippi is rural. Even the cities are rural."

They all stood for a time and watched the huge awful luminescent cross between a wrecked battle ship and a crashed jetliner that was their new modern city hall.

It did not speak to them.

And so Nina could only think back.

That trip to Lafayette.

The meeting with the CEO of Gulf Coast Petroleum.

Who happened, to Nina's great surprise, to be a woman!

The corporation's headquarters were housed in a building just as non-descript as any of the others in downtown Lafayette. There was nothing to distinguish it, save the letters GP etched primly in gray limestone above the doorway.

She was led through the door.

She and the tall blonde young man assigned to be her guide zigzagged though the ground floor of the building, rounding a deserted corner in what seemed to be a deserted hallway, entering a second elevator, and pushing a button for the second floor.

"Here we are. If you'll just step inside..."

A heavy door opened before her.

The office she found herself in resembled the inner sanctum of a cathedral. There was a great, stained glass window behind her desk—a window that might have come from any of the reliquaries of Chartres or Lourdes—and beatific light poured into the small room, making her appear as the Abbess of a nunnery as she bent, bespectacled, over what seemed to be ponderous account books.

A diminutive figure rose up out of the shadows, rounded the desk, and strode across the room.

"You must be Ms. Bannister."

"Yes."

"I'm Barbara Daring. I'm the Chief Executive Officer here at Gulf Coast Petroleum."

She could not, Nina estimated, have been more than four feet tall, but the most striking thing about her was her manner of crooking her head precisely at forty-five degrees (It seemed to be bent first one direction at forty five degrees and then another, without visibly making the transformation) and turning her head upon her neck at another precise forty-five degree revolution, so that she had the effect always of peeking outward and upward at the world from beneath an invisible fence.

But her smile…

The smile was perhaps more memorable than either stature or angularity. It was unchanging, unwavering, explosively, radioactively white. It took up half of her face, and exerted so much upward pressure that the eyes above it remained permanently squinted, small dark slits of mascara which ran down and away from her angular, slender, nose, at another forty-five degrees.

She kept her gaze fixed upward and crookedly on Nina, an amazing feat, Nina concluded, for a woman with no visible eyes.

She was a red and black woman, and ageless. There was too much makeup (also red and black) to perceive her skin, and too much brightness to examine her character or demeanor.

She could have been the governor's wife or a carnival ride.

"Nina—I hope I may be allowed to call you Nina?"

"Of course."

"Marvelous!"

Her pronunciation of the word "marvelous" would have been worth the price of a theater ticket.

It was a three generation pronunciation, and almost certainly a multi-continental one.

It was the kind of pronunciation that seemed to bend the speaker's body around it, inflate the soul responsible for it, and exalt humanity in general.

It was a pronunciation to be celebrated, if never fully comprehended.

"Thank you," said Nina, ineffectually.

"I took the liberty of reserving the small meeting room next door. Do you like caviar?"

This was an unanswerable question, or at least unanswerable as a yes or no question. 'Yes,' implied that one actually had the chance of eating caviar regularly, which, of course, was ridiculous, and 'no' was like answering 'no' to the question "Do you enjoy having sex?": vaguely unsporting, and, ultimately, a bit defeatist.

"I love caviar."

"Marvelous!"

Again! The Ziegfeld Follies and the Metropolitan Opera, bottled in tandem, and opened in an inner sanctum of one of the world's great oil companies!

"Let's go over then, shall we? Just right through here…"

Corridor corridor corridor corridor…

Door…

Unlock door, open door…

The windows, Nina estimated, must be a foot thick.

Either the oil industry did not like the outside world or it feared gunfire.

Or both.

There was a table in the center of the room. It was not particularly large, but it was solid and immovable. It was Odysseus's bed, hewn from the trunk of a massive tree and left in place for the building to grow around it.

"Please sit, Nina."

"Thank you."

"And so, Nina. I do know something of you, of your background. You were a teacher for a number of years, I believe."

"Yes. English teacher."

"I thought long and hard about going into teaching. Such a rewarding career."

"It has its good moments."

'I'm sure it does. I'm sure it does. As for myself, I hardly remember how I managed to wind up here. So many twists and turns."

"Were you in engineering?"

"For a time. Then business administration. Somehow the two worked their way together. And you reside now in Bay St. Lucy?"

"I do."

"How I envy you! I spent a delightful week there some years ago. I was staying with friends, but I still remember how perfect the beach was. And as for you—you were married to an attorney?"

"Yes, Frank. He passed away some years ago."

"I am sorry. I myself never married. Too involved in the job, I suppose."

"I suppose at the level you've reached, it's hard to have a personal life."

"It is. Some accomplish it; I wasn't able to."

They were silent for a time.

Then Nina knew it was time to get to the subject she had come about.

"I have to talk to you about..."

She was interrupted:

"About Mr. Cox. Yes, indeed."

"I guess I should start by telling you that I've known Paul all my life. In my opinion, he's..."

"He's an exceptional young man. I quite agree."

"You've found out some things about him?"

A nod.

"Oh yes. Yes, we received the unfortunate news about Congressman Thornbloom yesterday. And after your Mr. Bennett called one of our people, I was able to have some research done. We aren't the CIA, but we have our sources for gathering information."

"So what do you think?"

"About Paul Cox? One can only speak of him in positives. A young man, highly thought of in many circles in Jackson. A true reformer. Clearly, the man knows how to give a speech."

A pause.

Nina:

"But?"

Barbara Daring shook her head.

"Ms. Bannister, I'm now going to be telling you several things that I'm sure you already know. But I'm going to do so anyway. First, the coming election—not just this special election in March but the national election in November—is exceptionally vital in the history of our nation. It may, in fact, be the most vital election we have had. So many close battles, so many deep and bitter disputes, and so much riding on the outcome of every race, in every state. Control of the Senate, control of The House of Representatives—it all hangs in the balance."

"Yes. I'm aware of that. But I do think that Paul..."

"The long and short of it is that the winner of this election in March needs to be capable of winning in November. We aren't simply choosing a lame duck here. We need an exceptional person, who can keep going."

"I can promise you that Paul is such a person. At least, I believe he is."

"I'm sure he is. But, as I was saying, the interests of Gulf Coast Petroleum in these elections are huge. There are the questions of governmental regulations to deal with, of course; but more important are decisions that must and will be made about the Alaskan pipeline. Ms. Bannister, I will put this as succinctly as possible: our country can no longer afford to be dependent on oil from The Middle East. There is simply too much instability in the region. We are no longer certain that the people we are paying trillions of dollars to, are not converting that money into weapons to use against us."

Nina knew nothing to say to this.

She simply nodded.

Barbara Daring continued:

"At first glance then, it might seem logical that the corporation might wish to throw all its support behind a Republican candidate. The Democrats have in the past seemed more receptive to environmental issues, and more passionate about preserving the wilderness, etc. But Nina...I may call you Nina?"

"Of course."

"Nina, I'm not so certain that I want to base everything on party affiliation. That deep-rooted intransigence, that proclivity for saying 'Our party believes *x* and yours believes *y* and we never compromise. That proclivity is paralyzing our government, and, as a natural consequence, our nation."

"Yes. I read the papers. I know what's been happening in Washington. Or not happening."

"I'm sure you do read the papers. I'm certain that you read a great deal more than that. Which is why I'm telling you that Gulf Coast Petroleum wants to back a very special person in this election."

"And that's why I'm telling you that Paul will…"

"Hush, dear."

She did.

The woman opposite her continued:

"We need someone who can see beneath the stereotypes. We need someone who genuinely loves the environment—but who understands how deeply we care about it too. We need someone who can help us make the bridge between the environmental lobby and our research laboratories. Laboratories that, I might add, are fixated twenty-four hours a day on meeting the energy needs of the nation, but in doing so with absolute safety."

Another pause.

"Do you see what I'm saying, Nina?"

"Yes. I think I do."

Then a smile.

"Of course you do. You've already proven that you do. You already know how Aquatica runs."

"I thought I knew before I went out there. I thought you were all environmental villains."

"But you learned different."

"Yes. I learned different."

"And that is what, my dear, our candidate must be able to help the entire country to do. We must, in short, have a teacher representing us in Washington."

"But Paul *is* a teacher! If Paul can't do the job you've just described, who can?"

Barbara Daring simply continued to smile.

And Nina, finally, understood.

This woman was talking about her.

Within the week—because Jackson was nothing if not industrious—all necessary papers had been filed.

Nina Bannister was running for Congress.

Soon afterwards she found herself in an interior room of the Auberge des Arts, cameras focused on her, whirring lights shining in her eyes, and an audience of five people (Alanna Delafosse, Paul Cox, Jackson Bennett, Edie Towler, and Margot Gavin, who had driven down for the occasion) preparing to grill her with the kinds of questions she was sure to get in press conferences, and could also expect in the two statewide debates, the first of which was to take place March 7.

The cameras in front of her were actually taking pictures, just as they would be in a live press conference.

The microphones were actually recording.

This is the way that it would be.

Everything was ready.

She, dressed as a principal, wondered if, seated primly at a table and facing the audience, she looked like Hillary Clinton.

She was just wondering how she felt about that prospect when Paul rose from the first row and asked:

"You ready, Nina?"

She nodded.

What if she looked like Nixon?

"I'm ready."

"Remember. You're among friends here. Take your time with answers. You just need to be sure of your positions."

"I know."

"If we need to help you with research, we're all ready to do that."

"I know that, too, Paul. And I appreciate it."

"The main rule in this kind of thing is, don't pretend to know something if you don't. It's better just to say, 'I don't know.'"

"I understand."

"Ok."

He turned and looked at the group of people seated behind him, then asked:

"Who wants to ask the first question?"

Alanna Delafosse rose.

"Nina, darling."

"Yes?"

"What are your thoughts on the situation in the Middle East?"

She answered immediately:

"I think it's very bad there."

Silence for a time.

Alanna again:

"I suppose what we really want to know, Nina, is, how should the United States proceed in the Middle East? What should be our policy?"

Again, an immediate answer.

She had expected this question. And Jackson had told her precisely how it should be answered:

"I think we should do everything in our power to make the situation better."

General nods in the audience.

A buzzing of contented whispers.

Jackson said:

"That's the perfect answer. Never change a word of it."

But now Paul Cox was standing.

"How do you feel about prayer in schools?"

She thought about every morning, the bell between first and second period having just rung, a thousand teenagers disgorged into the hall, football players hurling themselves into lockers, the whole crowd stampeding toward her.

"I pray constantly in school. Every day. Every minute actually."

Jackson:

"Do you think the military is ready for women in combat?"

She thought of Penelope Royale and immediately answered:

"No."

Edie Towler:

"How do you feel about the legalization of marijuana?"

She began to answer.

"I don't think that…"

Then she saw Margot.

Margot was staring at her.

Margot's fingers were wrapped over the back of the chair just in front of her.

Then Margot half stood up and hissed out into the room—

"Nina!"

But Nina could only pause for a time and say, quietly:

"I think I better come back to that one."

Margot said:

"We'll talk."

And then sat down.

Edie:

"What do you think about gay marriage?"

She thought about Meg Brennan, one time women's basketball coach at Bay St. Lucy, and about Meg's companion Jennifer Warren.

How thrilled they had been when gay marriage had been legalized in New Mexico, and the joy in their eyes after they had returned from there, a married couple at last.

And she thought about the spousal abuse cases she read about daily, cases in which men beat and often killed their wives.

Finally she said:

"It is so hard to stop people from hating each other, that we have no business regulating the various ways they may find to love each other."

Silence for a time after that.

Then Edie again:

"Nina, how do you feel about abortion rights? Are you pro-choice or pro-life?"

Again, it was a question she had expected.

Indeed, she had answered it over and over to herself during the last few days.

And again, the images flooded back.

That day in the doctor's office when he had said, in the same way doctors earlier in her life had said, "Your tonsils are fine," or "You may have the measles."

"Nina, Frank, it pains me to say that you will not be able to have children."

And that was that.

So now to think that a woman could have a child in her womb, a growing child, the child that she and Frank would have given so much, so very much to have and raise...

...that that woman would wish to have an abortion...

But all women were not Nina; she knew that.

And horrible things sometimes happened to women.

Things that she, being blessed with Frank, would never be able to dream of.

So that finally she said, simply:

"I believe our job is not to tell women that they cannot have abortions, but to create a world in which they will not want to."

That ended the mock press conference.

There was nothing else to say.

Except there *was* one more thing to say.

And she said it the next afternoon.

Jackson had managed to set up an interview for her with the *Vicksburg Star* daily newspaper. Accordingly, a very professional woman—the reporter—had arrived at her shack, along with a photographer.

She was asked to sit on her deck, the ocean behind her, and she had prepared herself to answer what she had assumed would be standard questions. When there was a knock at the door.

She answered it to find Olivia Ramirez, mother of Edgar.

Edgar had been one of Nina's best students.

He had also been killed in a tragedy that still haunted Bay St. Lucy.

"Come in, Olivia!"

Olivia entered the shack.

"Oh! You have guests!"

"It's all right. This is a reporter from *The Vicksburg Star*. Come out on the deck, Olivia. Sit down in one of these chairs."

"I am so sorry to intrude."

"You're not intruding. Here. Sit."

She did so, with Nina taking the other chair.

The reporter and the photographer watched from the kitchen doorway.

"How may I help you, Olivia?"

The woman's hair and eyes were as black as her dress.

She leaned forward and said, softly:

"You will go to Washington?"

"I don't know. I'm going to try."

"If you try, Ms. Bannister, our teacher, you will succeed. Always, you succeed."

"I will try my best."

"Yes. Then, when you go there, I have something that I must beg you to do."

"All right. What is it, Olivia?"

The woman took a deep breath, folded her hands in her lap, and said, quietly:

"The children."

"I'm sorry?"

"From south of Mexico. They come. They are coming, to stay here."

"Refugee children, yes, I know. Many of them are coming up from Honduras."

"They are no different than my children. No different than Hector, and Edgar, and Sonia. And they are all alone. Hundreds of miles. They walk. Some of them die in the desert."

Nina could only nod.

"I know, Olivia."

"The people in Washington, they do nothing. Nothing! What is wrong with these people?"

"I don't know what is wrong with them."

"You will talk to them?"

"Yes. Yes, I will do that. I promise that I will do that."

There were tears shimmering in Olivia Ramirez' eyes, and her voice had begun to crack.

"There are children at our borders! Are we going to let these children die? What kind of people are we?"

And with that, Nina leaned forward, took Olivia's hands in her own, and said:

"I solemnly promise you. I will take care of these children. Whatever else I do, I will find a million mothers to help me. And if we have to *walk* down there, and *walk* back—we will take care of these children."

After that, silence for a time.

Only the growling of the waves and the gentle whirring of the camera.

Finally, Olivia Ramirez rose, apologized for interrupting the interview, and, still holding Nina's hand, made her way out of the shack and down the stairs.

When Nina got back to the deck, she found the photographer folding up his camera.

"What," she asked, "is he doing?"

The reporter was looking out over the deck.

"Getting ready to go back to Vicksburg."

"Why? What about the interview?"

"Useless. Useless."

"Why?"

"We just got the story of the decade. There's a Pulitzer, right there in the camera. Now all you and I and Jackson Bennett have to do is go back to work and be sure the country sees it."

And they did.

The tape of Nina's promise to Olivia Ramirez—along with the tape she had made in the Auberge des Arts—was shown hundreds of times in the following weeks.

No debates were necessary for Nina, and she did not participate in them.

She had stated her views eloquently, simply, and passionately.

Now it was the voters' decision.

And so it became midnight.

Then one a.m. on the day after the Special Election to choose Jarrod Thornbloom's replacement.

Nina had gone to sleep with her head lying on one of the tables in The Bay St. Lucy Town Hall.

She was awakened by the firm hand of Edie Towler shaking her by the shoulder.

It was Edie's face she saw when she first opened her eyes, and Edie's voice, solemn and quiet, that seeped into her consciousness:

"I'm sorry, Nina."

"What?"

"It's over."

"What time is it, Edie?"

"Just a little after one."

"I don't... I must have..."

"You dozed off."

"Where's everybody else?"

"They're outside."

"What happened?"

"The northern counties. The ones we were so unsure about. They've all reported in. Tallies are done."

"What happened?"

Edie simply shook her head.

"I'm sorry. I have bad news for you."

"Oh, no."

"Yes, there's not much we can do about it."

She could remember rubbing her eyes, already sleep-gummed, and looking around the strange gray vacant room, banners hanging like shrapnel after a mass attack.

"We fought a good fight, Edie."

"We certainly did."

"What's that roaring sound?"

Because there was a roaring sound.

It seemed to engulf the building.

"Fireworks, I think. All the yachts in the Bay St. Lucy harbor have formed a ring, and they're shooting fireworks over the city. If you come outside you can see."

And she had gone outside, Edie beside her.

And she had peered upward at the March sky, now lit garishly in shades of sky rocket.

"They're doing this for me?"

"Indeed they are."

"Bay St. Lucy. God I love Bay St. Lucy."

"I know. I know."

"How much did we lose by, Edie?"

Edie stared at her.

"What?"

"I said, how much did we lose by?"

"What are you talking about?"

"You said, 'I'm sorry, Nina.' When you woke me, you said, 'I'm sorry.'"

"I am."

"Then…"

"No more beachcombing for you. I'm sorry—but we're going to lose you for a while."

"You mean…"

"You won, Nina. By three hundred and fifteen votes. You're a member of The House of Representatives now.

"Well. What do you know about that?" she whispered.

They sky exploded above her.

And for the first time she realized:

Nina Bannister was going to Washington!

CHAPTER TWO: WELCOME TO WASHINGTON!

Precisely one week later, she arrived at Dulles International Airport, flown there by a private jet owned by Gulf Coast Petroleum.

She was met at the foot of the plane's exit ramp by a tall, thin fortyish man, whose broad smile showed creases around both eyes that had obviously been caused by much sunshine or much happiness.

Or perhaps both.

"Congresswoman Bannister!"

He stepped forward and held out his hand.

She took it, realizing that a photographer was standing just behind him.

Shake of the hand!

Pop! Goes the flashbulb!

And Nina is officially in the nation's capital.

"Congresswoman, I'm Dicken Proctor. I am—well, sorry to say, I was—Chief of Staff for Jarrod Thornbloom."

"I know, I know, and thank you for your emails! I'm sorry I didn't have time to answer all of your questions. It's just been chaotic. And I want to tell you how deeply sorry I am—and everybody in Bay St. Lucy is—about the Congressman."

"I know. It's unthinkable that something like this could have happened. The Congressman and I were quite close. We had worked together for ten years. I drove him to the airport on the morning of…well, suffice to say, I'm still in shock."

"They still don't know the cause of the crash?"

A shake of the head:

"Not yet. Given the area where contact was lost. It's very deep there. They found some wreckage but not the black box. And, of course, no way to recover the bodies."

Nina knew nothing to say.

Dicken Proctor continued:

"Working for Congressman Thornbloom wasn't always easy. He could be a difficult man. More so as he got older. But his heart was always in the right place; he fought passionately for the causes he believed in."

"I believe that," said Nina. "I really do."

Although, she did not say, *I think he may have been losing his mind and getting senile, and last November I voted for a Republican.*

No, that was not the thing to say.

"Well, I hardly know where to begin in introducing you to Washington."

"Anywhere you like."

"Come on then. We'll get your bags and go on outside. We have a car waiting for you. I've booked you a room at the Hotel George. It's not the most expensive hotel on the hill, but it's one of my favorites. From the higher windows—and you're on the fourth floor—you can see the capitol dome."

"Great!"

"When various dignitaries flew into town to meet with the Congressman, I always arranged for them to stay there, unless they specified somewhere else. I think you'll be comfortable there tonight—then tomorrow we'll set about getting you a real place."

"Lead the way."

He did, and the two bags that Nina had checked were soon picked up.

The limousine awaiting her oozed darkness and quietness and comfort, and she appreciated the touch of the bottle of water sitting primly and coolly in a special holder just in front of her knees as she slid into the back seat.

The ride into the city was difficult.

Dicken Proctor was an unending stream of information—information she should have already known, she told herself, but the week following her election victory had gone by so fast—and she knew she should have been paying complete attention to him.

But Washington was flowing by.

And she had never been there.

And there were cherry blossoms everywhere!

And there—they were approaching the Mall!

Now they had turned on Constitution Avenue.

It was all there to her right, flowing by:

The Lincoln Memorial.

Beyond that, the Korean War Veterans' Memorial.

And over beyond that, the Martin Luther King Jr. Memorial.

And there, there before them, now almost abreast of them—The Washington Monument!

So how could she listen, how could she talk, ask questions?

Still, somehow, she did.

"What will the first days be like?"

"Very very busy. One good thing is, we've already moved into the new office."

"I have a new office?"

"Well, you have a different office. Offices on the hill are a matter of seniority. The Congressman had been in office over twenty years, and so he had a pretty elegant place."

"And I?"

A shake of the head.

"Sorry. More like a boiler room. But we'll make out okay."

"And as for staffers?"

"You have eight, plus me. They're a good bunch. I think you'll like them."

"What do they do? What do I do, actually? Seems stupid to be asking a question like that. I won an election to Congress, and now I have no idea what to do with myself once I'm here."

"Don't worry about it. Everybody's confused at first. But the important thing is, get ready to do a lot of eating."

"Eating?"

"Eating. Nobody meets anybody on Capitol Hill unless there's a plate of food between them. And, of course, everybody wants to meet you. They would anyway, just out of politeness. But that campaign you ran…"

"Well, actually, it's the campaign Jackson Bennett ran."

"Maybe, but it was still remarkable. At any rate, you're scheduled to meet tomorrow with the House Minority Leader at ten, and there are other congressmen calling to get in whenever possible. These meetings won't last long; you just have to say *hello*."

"All right. But afterwards—I mean, what is a normal day like?"

He smiled.

My God! There, out the window beyond him, is the Smithsonian!

"Congresswoman Bannister."

"Nina, please. Just Nina."

"All right, Nina; I won't lie to you. A vast majority of your job is two things: answering letters—we get almost a thousand a week, and that's real letters, not just emails, of which there are five hundred more—and helping to raise money. In the autumn, the main business of Congress is to propose legislation. In the spring, the main business is to generate money, to pay for the legislation. You're already down for four fundraisers, one of which will require a trip back to Mississippi in two weeks. I'm sorry that I went ahead and said *yes* to these invitations, but…"

"No, no, it's exactly what you needed to do. I'll go wherever I'm needed."

"Excellent. But there's also the issue of where you're going to stay. I mean, permanently."

"You said in your last email that there were several possibilities?"

"There are. As you know, Congressman Thornbloom was a widower."

"Yes, I knew that."

"He lived by himself for the past eight years in a rather elegant townhome in Georgetown. But that has, in the last few days, been put on the market. We assumed it would have been somewhat difficult for you to live there."

"True."

"I've had several calls from your supporters, though—one of whom is a Ms. Daring."

"Barbara."

"Yes, the CEO of Gulf Coast Petroleum. She says that I'm to help you find a truly first rate-place, and not to worry greatly about the rent. So there are several things we can look at tomorrow."

"Excellent. I don't need much—I'm used to living in a two-room shack overlooking the gulf."

"You'll have several choices. Now, though, there is one more difficult matter I probably need to tell you about. I thought about waiting until next week, but…no, it's definitely something you should be told of as quickly as possible."

"What is it?"

"Well, as I mentioned a minute or so ago, congressmen get letters. No congressman can open and read and answer all of them. That becomes our job as staffers. We only show you the ones we feel to be truly important, or truly different."

"I understand."

"Occasionally there are crank letters. And some letters are obscene."

"That would follow, I guess. Not all people like politicians."

"No, they don't. If the letters are truly scary, then we pass them along to the Secret Service. Sometimes they can trace them, sometimes not."

"I take it, then, that I've been getting some scary letters."

"Yes. Two came to you last week, just after the election."

"You have them?"

"Here."

Both letters were typed on elegant, cream-colored stationery.

The first said:

Congresswoman Bannister:

I AM SORRY TO HAVE TO CONTACT YOU IN THIS WAY, BUT I HAVE NO CHOICE. I AM COMMANDED TO DO SO BY A HIGHER POWER. YOU MUST UNDERSTAND THAT THE POLICIES CURRENTLY BEING FOLLOWED BY YOU AND YOUR PARTY ARE PURELY EVIL. THEY ARE THE WORK OF THE DEVIL. RENOUNCE THEM IMMEDIATELY, OR THE DIVINE CREATOR WILL TAKE HIS REVENGE ON YOU!

"Well," said Nina, quietly, "that's pretty creepy. No way to trace it?"

"No."

"What policies does the divine creator hate so much?"

"I don't know. The Congressman was an advocate of gay marriage. Abortion rights. Legalization of marijuana. The basic liberal agenda. A lot of people don't like those positions."

"Right. So. The second one?"

"Here."

"Same stationary, looks like. When did it come?"

Dicken Proctor looked at her and said:

"This morning. It was in the mail this morning."

She read:

TO NINA BANNISTER:

YOU ARE AN EVIL WOMAN. RENOUNCE YOUR BELIEFS, OR YOU WILL NOT BE ALLOWED TO LIVE.

"Well, that's comforting."

"I'm sorry to have to show you these."

She shrugged:

"I assume that just goes with the territory. Any suspicious characters lurking around the Congressman's office before his accident?"

A smile:

"This is Washington, Nina. Sometimes I think nobody lives here *but* suspicious characters."

"Well. All I can say is, I'll keep my eyes open."

How did one do that, though? she found herself wondering, in a world of suspicious characters?

CHAPTER THREE: A MEETING AND A MENTAL
CONVERSATION

The following day, Nina had lunch at the House
cafeteria.

She had just finished the meal when she heard this
mellow, deep woman's voice coming from behind her,
over her shoulder.

"Congresswoman Bannister?"

(What it was like to be called that for the first time!)

"Yes?"

She turned around.

And there was Laurencia Dalrymple.

Laurencia Dalrymple!

One of the most famous of all senators.

Reputed to be the first black woman who would
make a run at the presidency!

Standing beside Nina's table.

"May I sit down?"

"Of course! Of course!"

"Congratulations on your victory!"

"Thank you! Thank you so much!"

"I adored your TV ads. And I wanted to come and
see you the first chance I got. I went by your office, and
your chief of staff told me they thought you were here.
You have, by the way, a very friendly chief of staff."

"Yes, Dicken Proctor. He loves two things: making
coffee and playing golf. I've never seen him play golf,
so I don't know if he's any good at that or not. But the
coffee? He's an expert. Our little office has the best
coffee-making equipment in the world, and Dicken

always arrives before everybody else to make a pot. He even had coffee thermoses specially made with the Mississippi flag painted on them. When anybody has to go to a meeting, he makes sure that person has one of those thermoses, and will not have to suffer through bad coffee."

"I'm so glad you're in good hands, my dear. But I did want to congratulate you. It's a privilege to have a career teacher as a colleague. And, also—somewhat selfishly—it's always good to have another woman to work with."

"How many women are in the House and Senate?"

Laurencia smiled and said:

"Now I get to act like a schoolteacher! Well, my dear, I believe I can answer your question. There are at present one hundred senators, total, twenty of whom are of our sex. In the House, the number is four hundred and thirty five total, seventy-nine of them being biologically akin to you and me."

"Well. We're making some progress, I suppose."

"I suppose. But, as I say, it is always wonderful to welcome another woman. But welcoming you was not my only reason in coming. I wanted to make a strange—well, suggestion to you. I hope it won't sound too forward."

'Please, go ahead."

"Would you be at all interested in having a roommate for a time?"

"I'm sorry?"

And then there was that smile again.

"I know. I feel like such a fool…"

"No, no, actually I was going looking for a place tomorrow. Mr. Proctor was going to show me some possibilities."

"So you might be interested in rooming with me?"

"Of course! I'm just surprised, though—I mean, you've been in the Senate for a good many years now…"

"I'm old, you mean."

"No, no. I'm just surprised you need a roommate!"

"Well, as it happens, I do. Not for too long, I don't think. But for several months. I'm not sure you know too much about my personal life, Nina…"

"Not as much as I should, given your stature."

"Oh, pish about that. But the fact is, I am a widow, as, I believe, are you."

"Yes."

"I've been sharing a very nice apartment, just off Massachusetts Avenue, with an old and dear friend. She works in international banking, though, and has just been offered a handsome promotion. They want her to go and manage their branch in Paris."

"Oh, my."

"Yes, it's impossible to turn down. Also, my daughter will be graduating from Georgetown at the end of this coming summer semester. She will probably move in with me for a time, while she thinks about future plans. But from now through early fall…well, I followed your race with such interest, and came to feel as though you were someone I admired so much…I thought perhaps…"

"I would love it!"

"Really?"

"Absolutely! It would be a great honor for me!"

"And for me, too, Nina. For me, too. The apartment is just east of the corner of 3rd and E Streets. It's quite close to the Capital, and to the Rayburn House Office Building, where your office is. It's on the third floor of a stately old Victorian mansion. From the big window in our living room we can see down onto Massachusetts

Avenue, and, beyond that, the Thurgood Marshall Federal Judiciary Building."

"It sounds perfect."

"I think you'll be comfortable there. There is, however, just one thing that may be an issue..."

"What?"

"I have a cat."

That evening, she went to the Lincoln Memorial.

It was around sundown.

The cherry trees were beginning to blossom.

She overheard a guide talking to a group of visitors about Lincoln's hands. They looked, he said, especially lifelike because they were based on castings done while he was president. The guide said people who knew sign language might recognize that the left hand was shaped like an *A* and the right hand like an *L*. No one knew whether that was done intentionally, but the sculptor, Daniel Chester French, did have a deaf son.

Then, of course, after the group left, Nina went over and read one of the two full speeches in the Memorial.

The Gettysburg Address was one, of course.

The other one...

...ah, yes, the other one.

The Second Inaugural Address.

Those last lines...

"If we shall suppose that American slavery is one of those offenses which, in the providence of God, must needs come, but which, having continued through His appointed time, He now wills to remove, and that He gives to both North and South this terrible war as the woe due to those by whom the offense came, shall we discern therein any departure from those divine attributes which the believers in a living God always ascribe to Him? Fondly do we hope, fervently do we pray, that this mighty scourge of war may speedily pass away. Yet, if God wills that it continue until all the wealth piled by the bondsman's two hundred and fifty years of unrequited toil shall be sunk, and until every drop of blood drawn with the lash shall be paid by another drawn with the sword, as was said three thousand years ago, so still it must be said 'the judgments of the Lord are true and righteous altogether.'

With malice toward none, with charity for all, with firmness in the right as God gives us to see the right, let us strive on to finish the work we are in, to bind up the nation's wounds, to care for him who shall have borne the battle and for his widow and his orphan, to do all which may achieve and cherish a just and lasting peace among ourselves and with all nations."

With malice toward none, with charity for all...
To bind up the nation's wounds...
"They always were you've favorite lines, weren't they?"

Silence for a time, then:

"I think you would be so proud of me."

More silence. Then:

"I used to think, for so long a time, that you and Mr. Lincoln would have been good friends.

I don't think that any more.

What I think now, is that you and Mr. Lincoln *are* close friends.

And I believe that with all my heart.

Good bye for now,

My beloved Frank."

CHAPTER FOUR: OOPS!

Nina's existence in Washington went from exciting (first week), to less exciting (second week) to boring (third week), to frustrating (fourth week).

She had begun her career as congresswoman priding herself on being the perfect little legislator.

She missed no votes, but always sprang to her feet and raced into the House Chamber every time the bell rang in her office. She missed no fundraisers, whether they be given by the Veterans of Foreign Wars, the Poultry Producers of America, or the Daughters of the American Revolution. She allowed no letter that arrived in her office to go unread, and she made sure that all letters were promptly replied to, a task made even more onerous by the fact that all the replies said pretty much the same thing, no matter what the issue was that happened to be talked about.

"We understand your concern arising from the issue of ('Paste issue in *here*'). We in this office, and in the Democratic Party, share your worry about the matter, and are doing everything possible to find a fast and equitable solution. It is, of course, a complex situation, and finding an answer that will not only stop the pain that constituents such as yourself are feeling now, but in the future as well, is the full-time job of all of us here on Capitol Hill who have the privilege of representing you. Rest assured, we take our responsibilities *very* seriously. You, the other citizens of ('Paste town or city in *here*'), and indeed the entire state of Mississippi, can rest assured that your voices are being heard, your concerns acted upon, and your ideas put into motion.

Once again, it is a pleasure to be entitled to act as your representative,

The Honorable Nina Bannister."

She estimated that, by May first, she had signed five thousand such letters.

That would have been bad enough.

Worse, though, was her gradual realization that she was not going to bring about any major changes, or any changes at all.

Nor was anybody else in Washington.

The government, of which she was now a part, was at a standstill.

Republicans hated Democrats, who hated them right back.

There was no compromise on anything.

And as Nina watched the train wreck that was the current congressional session…

…as she watched the inability of anyone to bridge the gap between various philosophies concerning gun control…

…health care reform…

…abortion rights issues…

…foreign policy issues…

…environmental and energy issues (She was failing Gulf Coast Petroleum, for whose causes she could do absolutely nothing)…

…and above all (she thought often of Ms. Ramirez) immigration reform…

…a strange and disturbing theory began to develop in her mind.

She tried to chase it out, but it remained there.

Where it grew.

Watching the people around her, and how they behaved toward each other and their adversaries, she began to feel that the major polarity dividing the nation had nothing to do with conservative vs. liberal thought.

It had much more to do with…

…could she say it?

Could she ever put into words exactly why she felt the nation was paralyzed politically?

No. To do so would be disastrous for her, and for her party.

She would be laughed out of Washington.

And so she should never say what she was truly feeling.

Except, one day, she did.

It happened as follows:

Her slip occurred in a second interview with the young woman from *The Vicksburg Star* who had recorded her interview with Olivia Ramirez.

This reporter had called a week after her arrival in Washington, anxious to do a backup story.

And Nina had agreed.

Why not?

And so on Thursday, May third, she found herself in the coffee room of her cramped office (There were in all, three rooms: the reception room, which swarmed with aids; the coffee room, where there was Proctor's wonderful coffee, a table, and four chairs; and her inner sanctum, where there was a massive desk and an uncomfortable couch facing it, all such offices having uncomfortable couches, she was to learn, because congress people wanted always to give constituents an obvious place to sit, and never to have them stay very long.)

She found herself in this middle room, sipping coffee, looking alternately at the trim, dark-haired reporter and the massive Confederate battle flag that stretched across the wall over the doorway.

"So, you've been here a month now, Representative Bannister?"

"Please call me Nina. I'd like you to call me that, and I'd like all Mississippians to call me that. I'm just Nina."

"All right then, Nina. How have you adjusted to life on the Hill?"

"I love it."

"What things about it most specifically?"

"Well, I think the chance to interact with so many folks around the state."

"How does this interaction take place?"

"Mainly through letters and emails. I have flown back to Jackson on two occasions to attend party fundraisers, and I loved, as a kind of addendum to the second trip, being given a tour of the huge chicken processing plant outside of Oakdale. Genuinely fascinating. But having a chance to sit down and answer each letter personally—that's *so* gratifying!"

"Wonderful! Well, then—I think our readers would enjoy knowing what aspect of Washington D.C. has impressed you most?"

"There are so many, Elizabeth! But I have to say, not even all of the amazing monuments, and all of the history—not all of these things can move me as much as the cherry blossoms can. I'm a small town Mississippi girl at heart, and when I look out of the Capitol Dome over this sea of white and pink—I can't tell you how deeply it moves me."

"I'm sure every Mississippian wants to be right there with you."

"In a way, I feel as though they are with me."

"How moving! Nina, has it been difficult as a woman, getting things accomplished on Capitol Hill?"

"Not at all. There are, as you know, a number of other women representatives and senators—I have the great pleasure of rooming now with Senator Laurencia Dalrymple—and I don't think any of my colleagues see gender as an issue when it comes to solving the nation's problems."

"Speaking of that, then, what are the problems that you find most vexing?"

CORRECT ANSWER:

"Oh, I think they're the same ones that you and your subscribers read about every day. We all want to find ways to help the President in his fight to improve the economy; we all want to aid those in our country who are less fortunate than ourselves; we're all concerned about the war-torn Middle East and the unstable situation in parts of Africa...and we want to find ways to decrease the violence that is plaguing our city streets, and costing so many young lives unnecessarily."

This was, inexplicably, not the answer that Nina gave.

She instead gave the:

INCORRECT ANSWER:

Partially because she saw, ever so briefly, a vision of Olivia Ramirez standing before her.

"We have fifty-thousand children pouring out of Latin America, looking for refuge in our country. They're children, Elizabeth. They're ten and twelve years old. They're dying. In the desert. At our doorstep. And we're doing nothing about it, except calling each other names."

"What should we be doing about it, Nina?"

EXTENSION OF INCORRECT ANSWER:

"Take them in."

"All fifty thousand?"

"There are three hundred million of us. Three hundred million. And we can't find homes for fifty thousand refugee kids? That would mean that, out of every sixty thousand Americans, one of them would need to take a child. One out of every sixty thousand would need to make that sacrifice. And we can't do that?"

And that was the end of the incorrect answer.

Except that it wasn't.

Fallout did not come immediately.

The evening following Nina's interview was, on the other hand, extremely pleasant. She was invited out to dinner with Laurencia Dalrymple, who took her to the Belga Café. She had never experienced Euro-fusion, which hinted vaguely at nuclear war, but she was game for anything (if, she sometimes found herself thinking, she were not game for anything, she would hardly be in Washington), and she went.

What a marvelous place!

A sleek café, done up with dark wood, exposed brick walls, and spotted with creamy chairs, elegant linen.

An endive salad with a sabayon made from Hoegaarden beer.

Where for an hour or so, they simply sat, and munched, and sipped, and watched the Capitol Dome grow brighter as the sky beyond the restaurant's huge windows darkened.

Over a three shellfish gumbo, they traded tales of their childhood.

Over a fluffy taramosalata (salmon roe dip) with a touch of citrus, they traded tales of their husbands.

Over salty halloumi cheese topped with mint, they traded tales of scandal and intrigue involving various legislators and their mistresses, and, since gender equity was in fact becoming a reality, their misters.

And over apple pie and coffee (one could take eclecticism only so far), they simply digested, and talked of nothing at all.

Nina slept like a rock.

Astonishingly, she was hungry the next morning when she woke at six-thirty.

She ate her accustomed bagel with cream cheese (Where was she putting all this food?), dressed, walked to the office, greeted her staffers as they came smiling in, and had answered forty-three letters when the messenger came for her at nine-fifteen.

Later on, she could remember the time because she had just glanced at the Ole Miss clock with the rebel flag hanging down from it, when the man arrived.

He looked out of place among her own staffers: a bit older, a bit less blond, a bit crooked, and a bit too well dressed for basement offices or basement people.

"Could I see Congresswoman Bannister?"

"She's in the coffee room."

She was not in the coffee room, however. She was, in fact, standing flush in the doorway between the entrance room and the coffee room.

"I'm Congresswoman Bannister."

"Good morning. I'm Tim Sandler, aide to Jeb Maxwell."

Jeb Maxwell.

The House Whip.

Second in line, at least in terms of the power structure, to the Minority Leader.

"Ah! And how may I help Congressman Maxwell?"

A slight blush.

A deferential bow.

Then:

"Well, he hates to interrupt your morning. He knows you probably have a million things on your plate."

"That's true. Right now I'm ending nuclear war and in a minute or so I'm going to set about eliminating disease and poverty."

Ha ha ha.

Ha ha ha.

"No, seriously…"

Be quiet, Nina.

Stop acting like an idiot.

"Seriously, I'm always at the Congressman's service."

"Wonderful. Do you think you could spare a few minutes now?"

"Sure."

So she got her jacket and followed Tim Sandler up and out of the Rayburn Building, across South Capitol Street, through the Longworth House Building, across New Jersey Avenue, and into the Cannon House Office Building, where senior-level House administrators (and the Whip was certainly one of those) had their offices.

Along the way, he chatted pleasantly with her.

The talked about the weather.

Beautiful day. Beautiful day.

Certainly is. Certainly is.

The Gulf Coast.

Wonderful country down there.

Certainly is. Certainly is.

The fast pace of life in Washington D.C.

Are you getting used to it?

Little by little.

Ha ha ha.

Ha ha ha.

Then they took the elevator up to the third floor, walked along a corridor for eight or nine miles, and stopped before a massive oaken door.

"Have you been in Congressman Maxwell's office before, Congresswoman Bannister?"

"No, I haven't."

"And you haven't yet met the Congressman?"

"No."

"Well, I'll introduce you!"

He opened the door.

The room flashed and glittered and laughed and sun-sparkled and was just completely happy about everything in the whole damned world.

It was a massive room, surrounded with massive windows, which let in wondrous amounts of morning sunlight.

In the room were perhaps a dozen people, all chatting, all friendly to each other.

They all waved at her and greeted her as she stepped into the room.

She filtered through them and below them (for they were all taller than she was—even the furniture was taller than she was), and she shook as many hands as possible.

Finally, she came to rest standing before a man taller than anyone else. A man with white thinning hair, and a deeply chiseled face. He looked down at her with bright sparkling eyes and smiled:

"Tim, have you brought us Congresswoman Bannister?"

"Yes, sir, I have."

"Wonderful! May I call you Nina?"

"Of course!"

"Nina, I'm Jeb Maxwell."

"I know. I recognize you from TV!"

"And I have to apologize."

"For what, sir?"

"Why, for not coming round to your office much earlier, and making it my business to meet you. It's inexcusable on my part that it's taken this long!"

"Don't think anything of it."

"I think a great deal of it. That campaign you ran down there—absolutely marvelous work!"

"Well—most of it was Jackson Bennett's work."

"I know; I know Jackson. He's highly thought of up here. Good man, good man. But you more than did your part in that campaign. And to have had so little experience—the stuff dreams are made of. Dreams and movies. No, you're to be congratulated, no ifs ands or buts about it!"

"Thank you!"

"And now—look, you have to excuse me for just a second; we're finishing up a press conference. Want you to meet a few of these people. Here's Connie Hightower from NBC News…"

"Hi!"

"Hi!"

"Peter van Armstead, Reuters…"

"Hi!"

"Hi!"

"This is Senator Danielson from the House Armed Services Committee. Tom's come to give these press types an update on the P-345. You familiar with it?"

"No."

"Well, I'll send over some info on it. Interesting piece of equipment. Oh, and here's Dan Remmington, Ways and Means."

"Nice to meet you, Congresswoman Bannister!"

"Pleasure's mine."

"Helluva campaign. We all followed it. We loved Jarrod Thornbloom you understand…"

"Of course."

"But if there has to be a replacement—well, the state of Mississippi couldn't have done any better!"

"You're kind to say so."

"He's not just being kind," Jeb Maxwell interrupted. "It's the undeniable truth. Oh, and here you need to meet…"

So, for five minutes—it seemed much longer—she was herded through the room, given a chance to shake hand with this luminary or that lawmaker, this writer or that analyst, this TV talk show host or that retired general.

And always the talk of her wonderful campaign.

She was flattered, of course.

It was a remarkable thing.

She, little Nina Bannister.

Being fawned over by some of the most influential people in the world.

How many lunches of fish sticks and tater tots had she eaten in her life?

Now she was caviar lady.

Finally, the crowd oozed out of the room, and she was alone with Jeb Maxwell and his aide.

"Tim, I'm gonna go in the conference room back here with Congresswoman Bannister. See that we're not disturbed, will you?"

"Of course, sir."

"Now, Nina. If you'll come in here, maybe we can finally be alone."

"Sure."

And, so saying, he led her into his office and closed the door behind her.

"Sit down."

"All right."

The massive desk, of course.

And, damned if it wasn't true…

…the couch was uncomfortable.

"So, how are you finding Washington?"

"A bit fast pace, but I'm learning."

"Hear you're rooming with Laurencia Dalrymple."

"That's right."

"Remarkable lady."

"I think so."

"She may run for president, you know."

"I've heard that."

"And yet she's so down home, charming, but so easy to talk to."

"I know."

"So what the hell is this?"

A pause.

"I'm sorry…"

"I would think you're sorry. You damned well ought to be sorry!"

"I just…I don't…"

"You don't, huh! Well, look!"

He slid open a drawer of the desk, reached inside, and pulled out a newspaper.

The Washington Post.

He held up the front page.

There she was, lower right quarter of the page.

A picture of Nina Bannister.

And the headline:

"Dem. Lawmaker Advocates Blanket Welcome for Refugees!"

"I…I…"

"You haven't read this yet, Nina?"

"No. I didn't see the paper this morning. I've been answering mail."

"Read it."

He threw it at her.

She caught it and read:

"In a sharp break from party policy…"

She looked up.

"A sharp break from party policy is not good, is it?"

The face across from her, now brutally cold, glared back.

She forced herself to go on reading.

"In a sharp break from party policy, a junior member of the Democratic Party told a reporter yesterday that she favors allowing admission into the United States of all Honduran refugee children. 'There are only about fifty thousand of them,' said Congresswoman Nina Bannister, newly-elected representative from the state of Mississippi. 'And there are three hundred million Americans. That means only one American out of every fifty thousand would have to take in a child. Surely we can do as much!'"

She put down the newspaper.

"I didn't give this story," she said quietly, "to *The Washington Post*."

"If you give it to one paper, you give it to all of them. Surely you're not so stupid that you didn't know that."

The word stung, but there was nothing to do but sit and take it.

"And surely you also know that we are feverishly trying to work out a deal with the other side to fix this mess before it gets any worse. The President has asked for thirty billion dollars so that we can process these people and get them back home to where they came from. The Republicans are holding tough. All they can do is say, 'Why didn't you build the wall when you had the chance?' Right. A Berlin Wall right on our own border, built to keep people out and not in. Most ridiculous thing I ever heard of in my life. No. No, the most ridiculous thing I ever heard of in my life is you shooting off your damned mouth to the national media. And doing it without consulting a single member of your own party."

A horrible silence for a time.

There was no sound in the room, nor outside of it.

The Capitol Dome gleamed white through a huge window to her right.

It seemed to be grinning at her.

"The President is livid."

"The President knows about this story?"

Jeb Maxwell shook his head:

"No, of course not. The President never reads any newspapers. He especially doesn't read stories about his own party members making policies he's never heard of. But don't worry about him. He's heading off to Geneva later this morning for talks concerning the Ukraine. Oh, and by the way, I don't suppose you've thought of a way to solve that crisis too? Maybe just invite all the Ukrainians to come and stay at your place for a while? Maybe just a few years, until the Russians stop shooting at them?"

"Sir, I..."

"Lady, what in the hell were you thinking?"

More silence.

Deeper silence. Purple silence.

Then black silence.

She could only shake her head and whisper:

"I guess I wasn't thinking."

The black silence darkened.

She felt like a badly-behaved freshman who had been summoned to the principal's office.

Only that would have been for some minor offense such as fighting or breaking a window.

She had humiliated herself before the President of the United States.

And the question continued to lie there on the table like a dead seagull.

What had she been thinking about?

Well—

Olivia Ramirez for one.

But Olivia Ramirez was half a continent away right now.

Olivia Ramirez did not have to deal with the stark realities of Washington life.

"No, Ms. Bannister, the President is the least of your worries right now. The House Minority Leader is fuming. I've had calls from about twenty people, congressmen, senators...they're all asking me what drugs you're taking. By the way, you're not on drugs are you?"

She shook her head.

"No. I'm not on drugs."

"Damn. That would be an easy explanation. Then all we would have to do is get you into a rehab program and we could forget the whole thing. But there's no rehab program for stupid."

That word again.

Still, nothing to do about it.

"What do you want me to do?"

He shook his head:

"The best thing you can do is not to have given this story. No one on Capitol Hill—no one—favors simply opening up our border to any child who wants to wander up to it, and saying 'We'll find you a nice American family to spend ten years or so with, until we can get you into Harvard Law School.' Do you understand that?"

"Yes, sir."

"Most of the people calling me want your head. The problem is, there are more than twenty of them—by nine thirty, that is—and you've only got one head. So that's out."

She said nothing.

"There are various things we can do when congressmen—or women—speak out of turn."

"What are they?"

"Shoot them. Drown them. Send them off on a fact-finding tour somewhere. Make them Ambassador to France."

Nothing to say to that.

"But the truth is, we can't punish you."

"Why not?"

'You're too little. And you're a woman. And you're new. And you're from Mississippi, which means you've got three strikes against you right there when it comes to human intelligence. No, whatever we did—at least in public—it would look like we were bullying you. The National Society for the Protection and Preservation of Small, Inexperienced Southern Women would be up in arms."

She found this amusing, but she did not speak.

She had decided, actually, never to speak again.

Nor ever to leave her apartment again.

That would be the ticket!

A little boring, but much better than this.

"No, there is one thing you can do, and you have to do it, and you have to do it quick."

"And that would be?"

"Apologize. You have to hold a press conference. This afternoon."

"How do I…"

'Don't worry about it; it's all set up. It will be here in my office. There will be about fifteen reporters, all the usual crowd. Some of them you just met. Associated Press, Reuters, CNN. Anyway, you'll start the press conference by reading a statement that is already being prepared for you. Then you'll leave."

"But if they have questions…"

"They will have questions and you won't answer them. You'll just dammit leave. And that will be the last that anyone hears from the esteemed REPLACEMENT representative from the great state of

Mississippi for the rest of your stay in Washington. Do I make myself clear?"

"Yes, sir."

"All right. Now. You need to go with Tim. He'll take you somewhere private where you can have lunch and be certain not to be seen. He'll bring you back here at two. You'll have a chance to read over the statement you've going to make. Understand?"

"Yes."

"All right. Now please leave."

He rose, walked around his desk, and showed her out the door.

Certain moments are so wretched that they cannot be lived away from. Certain moments are so bleak and rotten that they do not serve as jumping off points for the future.

There is nothing to do after them.

Her conversation with the House Minority Whip constituted such a moment for Nina Bannister.

Looking back months and even years later, she could not remember doing anything from ten in the morning—when she had been called 'stupid' two or three times—until two in the afternoon, when her press conference was to take place.

Certainly, Tim Sandler was a part of her existence in this vacuum/vortex of non-being of having anything to live for except humiliation.

He must have taken her somewhere; then he must have bought her lunch.

Which she must have either eaten or left on the plate.

He must have chatted with her.

He was very good at chatting.

She, when one actually thought about it, was getting pretty good at chatting herself.

And he must have taken her back to Jeb Maxwell's office.

For that was where she found herself at two o'clock.

Having arrived fifteen minutes earlier, and having read the statement that had been typed out neatly and handed to her.

She stood at a podium.

Fifteen news reporters sat in three rows of folding chairs in front of her.

She did not have the courage to look at all of their faces.

Their faces were not important.

She had been told years before, in elementary school, that a good way to avoid being nervous while speaking before a crowd was to imagine all of the people in the crowd were wearing nothing but their underwear.

She had tried this once or twice, found it utterly disgusting, and given it up.

Now though, as she began reading, she could not avoid the feeling that *she* was wearing nothing but her underwear.

Well, so be it.

Underwear lady.

Nothing for it but to begin:

"Ladies and gentlemen, I am, as I'm sure you know by now, Congresswoman Nina Bannister."

Some small laughter at this.

It helped.

She continued.

"Yesterday I gave an interview with a reporter from a newspaper in my home state of Mississippi. This story was carried on the AP wire and ultimately appeared this morning in *The Washington Post*."

Everyone in the audience had laptop computers, the keyboards of which could be heard tapping away.

"I was not misquoted in this story, nor can I blame the reporter for what was in the story. She wrote down quite accurately what I said. What I must do now, however, is apologize. My statements did not reflect my actual feelings on the matter of the refugee children, nor did they accurately portray the views of the President, or the Democratic Party. I meant to say, and should have said, that in a perfect world, it would be wonderful if all American families could simply open their homes to the refugees of the world. It is not, however, a perfect world, and both major political parties realize this. They are, as we speak here today, attempting to find some compromise position that will allow us to deal humanely with the flood of children who are now standing at our borders. The President has made an urgent request for funds so that we can process these young people, and get them safely back to their families. But neither my party nor I really believe that it would be possible for us as a nation to offer them a blanket invitation to come and live in our homes. Our doing so would open up a flood of immigration that no nation could possibly withstand, or deal with. Once again, I apologize for having put my feelings so awkwardly, and having, because of my inexperience in public speaking, caused embarrassment to my party and to my President."

Silence for a moment.

Then:

"That is the end of my statement."

A sea of hands shot into the air.

"Congresswoman Bannister, do you..."

"Congresswoman Bannister, is it your..."

"Congresswoman Bannister, have you ever..."

Jeb Maxwell was approaching from the right of the podium:

"The Congresswoman, as I said before the press conference began, will not be..."

But then came a voice from the back of the room.

"Nina!"

A figure stood.

A tall woman.

With black-rimmed glasses.

"Nina!"

"I'm sorry, but…"

"I'm Liz Cohen of the *New York Times*."

Jeb Maxwell:

"Thank you for flying down, Ms. Cohen. We're all aware of your articles on behalf of Ms. Bannister during her campaign. I'm sure she appreciates your…"

"Nina?"

A pause.

Everyone was looking at her.

She was looking at Liz.

And she said:

"Yes, Liz?"

"Nina, do you believe the statement you just read?"

More silence.

A thousand one, a thousand two…

And finally she heard herself saying:

"No."

There was a collective gasp from everyone in the room.

The rattling of laptop keypads became deafening.

Everyone was typing and whispering into iPads simultaneously.

She was, she knew, being recorded.

At her shoulder, she heard the voice of the minority whip, saying quietly:

"What are you doing? You've got to…"

But she ignored the voice and went on speaking, while she looked directly at Liz.

"No, Liz. No. It was a statement written for me. But I don't believe a word of it. What I do believe is, we ought to take those children into our homes. We can do it. We should do it. And every one of you typing into your computers knows we should do it. The President knows it. The Congress knows it. And yet we sit up here like we're paralyzed. The whole government is paralyzed. We're in our own little entrenched positions, and the world is going to hell around us, and we can't compromise on anything. Not one damned thing. We are the most useless congress our nation has ever had. We are not 'binding up the nation's wounds' as President Lincoln told us to do. We're not binding up the world's wounds, either. We seem to have malice toward all, and charity toward none. Charity toward none. Fifty thousand children. Children, Liz! And all we can do is squabble about how to send them away most quickly."

She stopped talking.

The room was staring at her.

Jeb Maxwell had become a statue.

Finally, Liz said, quietly:

"Thank you, Nina. Thank you for telling the truth. Do you have anything further to say?"

Nina nodded:

"Yes."

"Then please do."

"All right. It's just this:"

She took a deep breath.

"It is with deep regret that I must take this occasion to announce my resignation from the United States House of Representatives."

And, so saying, she left the podium.

The shock in the room was great enough that a kind of paralysis set in. This state of motionlessness did not last long—a few seconds, at most—but it gave Nina a chance to hurtle through the door and out into the corridor.

She had disappeared from view before anyone could follow her.

Within two minutes, she was standing back in her own office, her own staffers standing around her.

They were all there, except Dicken Proctor, who was in Mississippi at a fund raiser.

A bad time, she found herself thinking, *for him to be away.*

"Listen, all of you. There's something I have to tell you."

Dutiful children, they sat with blank faces.

"I've just resigned. I'm going home to Mississippi."

More gasps.

She was eliciting a lot of gasps these days.

The inevitable questions.

What happened?

Is it something we've done?

Are you all right?

Who will replace you?

To all of these questions, she simply shook her head.

And then she lost it.

Looking back at the matter, she was surprised that she was not crying.

The old Nina would have cried.

This was not, of course, the old Nina.

This was angry Nina.

She was angry to recall how she had, in fact, wasted a month of her life.

Wasted it signing prewritten letters that said nothing.

Wasted it attending meetings in which nothing was accomplished.

Wasted it attending fund raisers, which did, in fact, raise money.

Money which did not seem to get put to any actual use.

For the speech she had just given was exactly right.

The government of which she had been a member up until a few minutes ago, was paralyzed.

The Republicans had their positions, from which they would not move.

Ever.

The Democrats had their positions, from which they would not move.

Ever.

With the result that thousands of children were left to starve in the desert.

"Okay," she found herself saying. "OK, guys, you've all worked hard to make this an easy transition for me. And I appreciate it. The reason I'm resigning has nothing to do with you. The reason I'm resigning has everything to do with this—this mess, that the government has gotten itself into. And I'm going to bare my soul to you. I'm going to tell you what I actually believe. I started believing it, I guess, when I met with Barbara Daring, the CEO of Gulf Coast Petroleum. I kept on believing it while I was getting to know Laurencia Dalrymple, who deserves to be our next president. I kept on believing it when I realized that Liz Cohen was the only person in an entire roomful of 'writers' and 'analysts' who really wanted to hear—and tell—the truth."

Pause.

"Do you know why this entire mess has come about?"

Silence.

"Men. Only about a fifth of our government is women. And that's better than it ever has been. For three thousand years, a hundred percent of our government—and every other government in the world—has been men. And the result? History is one big war. Men killing men by the thousands. By the millions. Men creating incredibly complex weapons so they could slaughter each other."

Pause.

"Women would not do this. Women would find a way to compromise. That is what women do—we find a way. We work it out."

Open mouths in the circle of staffers.

A few nods.

Mostly by the female staffers.

It was as though someone else was talking.

But it was Nina.

And she kept on.

"Do any of you think that a United States government run by women would let those children perish out there in the desert? Don't you believe it. Yes, there are women in this country who side with Republican values and others who side with Democratic values—but we all value more than anything else, human life. Because women bring life into the world. We scream and suffer so that people may come to be."

And now a few more nods.

And a few voices.

"Tell it."

"That's right."

"Do you people know the central difference between men and women? For women, the major metaphor of life is the maternity ward; for men the major metaphor of life is the battlefield. We, along with God, put people together; they, in spite of God, tear people apart."

"Yes!"

"Yes!"

"And *they* are governing *us*? Why? Why are we allowing this? WE OUTNUMBER THEM! What is the matter with us? Do you realize that the Senate just passed a bill to appropriate over a trillion dollars to continue work on a warplane THAT WON'T FLY! And if it ever does fly, all it will do is kill people and blow up buildings. No government run by women would ever be that insane! Listen! Listen to me!"

The circle moved in tighter.

"I'm sure that none of you have ever read Aristophanes. But you should. You should, in particular, read a play by him entitled *Lysistrata*. This is a play that takes place during the Peloponnesian War, the awful slaughter that lasted decades and almost destroyed the great city states of Athens and Sparta. Lysistrata and a group of Athenian women finally get sick of it. They get sick of losing their husbands and their young male children. So they meet secretly with a group of Spartan women who believe just like they do. And all of them say 'enough.' We're going to stop this war that the men have concocted! We're going on a SEX STRIKE until they stop the war! From now on, we're going to run things!"

Silence.

And finally, Nina knew that there was nothing more to say.

Except:

"That isn't going to happen. I know. There are too many men who feel like it's God's plan for them to run things. And, I guess, there are too many women who agree. We won't see sanity in our lifetime. Look. I've got to go now. I feel like I'm going to cry, and I don't want to. What I want to do is go somewhere and hide. There will be a lot of people here from the press in not very many minutes. If some of you could get my things together and put them in one place, I'd appreciate it. I'll sneak back tonight late and pick them up. For now, though, so long. And thanks for everything."

So saying, she left the office.

CHAPTER FIVE: THE POWER OF SOCIAL NETWORKING

She had covered half the distance between the Capitol Building and her apartment when the cell phone in her purse began to buzz.

She flipped it open and wondered for a second how she should answer the call.

Congresswoman Bannister?

She wasn't a congresswoman anymore.

Ms. Bannister?

That sounded too much like a principal.

And she wasn't one of those anymore, either.

Nina?

Somehow she didn't feel very 'Ninalike' at the moment.

So she simply said:

"Yes?"

"Nina, this is Laurencia."

Well, that was all right.

If there was one woman left in the world who she would allow to call her 'Nina'...

"Hello, Laurencia."

Pause.

"Nina, I saw your speech. Everyone, actually, has seen your speech."

"Well, I just..."

"No, no. We can talk about the speech later. More crucial now is that you not come back here to the apartment."

"Why not?"

"It's being circled by reporters. And the mob is growing."

"What should I do?"

"Get a cab. There should be quite a few on the street now. A lot of people are going home. At any rate, tell the driver to take you to 234 Barrington Drive."

"What is there?"

"A small hotel. Barrington Drive is in Foggy Bottom. This hotel is a Bistro Hotel, used by a good many of my friends when they wish to have illicit affairs."

"Why don't I just go to the Watergate while I'm at it?"

"No time to banter now, honey. Look, I'll try to get some food together and bring it over to you. You like sushi?"

"It's dead fish."

"I know. I thought it might be appropriate."

"Thank you."

"Just a bit of gallows humor."

"Thank you again. But Laurencia, I have to ask you before I get whisked off into hiding…"

"Yes?"

"I mean, why is this a big deal? I made a resignation speech. I'm the least important of all congressmen and women. People resign all the time. The truth of the matter was, I simply didn't believe the statement they gave me to sign. I know. Party loyalty and all that. But when Liz asked me that question…I don't know…I just had to tell the truth."

Pause.

Then:

"What question?"

"What do you mean, 'what question?' She asked me if I believed the statement I had just read. And I realized that, in all honesty, I didn't. So I said so. I also realized that I couldn't go around trumpeting views that went contrary to those of the president and my own party. So I had to resign. And I did."

Another pause.

"My God. You don't…"

"I don't what?"

The sound of Laurencia's breathing.

"Just get the cab, honey. Just get the cab, get into the hotel, and wait for me."

And she hung up.

Nina waited for her cab at Franklin and 12th, an intersection she knew to be quite busy.

The wait lasted approximately three minutes.

During the first minute, she was recognized by an elderly woman—stooped, caned, and white haired, but with sparkling blue eyes.

The woman grabbed her sleeve, smiled, and said:

"Saw your speech, my dear. Good for you. Stick by your principles."

"Thank you."

This kind of thing happened twice more.

Each time, it involved people telling her to stick to her principles.

She got the cab, gave the address, and tried to think of nothing while the driver negotiated afternoon Washington traffic.

The effort to think of nothing failed, since the driver recognized her too.

"You are Congresswoman Bannister?"

"Well. I was."

"I was able to see and hear your speech some time ago. I am Pakistani, you know. In my country, shame to say it, people cannot express their opinions as openly and frankly as you can here. Congratulations on the speech. How very powerful. Please, always stick to your convictions!"

"Thank you. That means a lot."

"You are welcome."

And he dropped her at the hotel.

It was small. Not at all ostentatious, but clean.

The desk clerk smiled and asked:

'How may I help you?"

"I need a room for the night."

"Will that be for only one?"

"Yes. I'm not having an affair."

"That's all right, madam; it isn't a requirement."

"Whew."

"Your name?"

"Nina Bannister."

"Ah! I heard your speech. Very moving."

"Thank you."

"No luggage?"

I might as well just admit, she found herself thinking, *that I'm having an affair.*

And who in this town hasn't heard that damn speech?

What do they do here besides watch television?

Of course, she thought, wishing for a bag of some kind to take upstairs, *what does anybody do besides watch TV?*

She was about to find out.

The room was fine.

A bed, well made, to be slept on.

A writing desk to be…

…what?

Whoever, she wondered, *ever went to a hotel to write things?*

Twenty minutes later, Laurencia arrived, with an overnight bag full of gear for Nina to sleep in, and a large box of pizza.

Laurencia smiled:

"Canadian bacon and pineapple. That all right with you?"

"It's great, especially because they allow you to pick off the pieces of pineapple."

"So. A traditionalist."

"Damned straight. Let's eat."

Nina took the box and opened it, savoring the aroma.

"This is the highlight of my day, Laurencia. Of course, it doesn't have much competition…"

In a minute, the two women were sitting on the bed and chowing down.

Nina:

"Now will you please tell me…"

Chomp chomp..

"How does everybody know about my resignation speech?"

Laurencia shook her head:

"Nobody knows about your resignation speech. I don't even know about your resignation speech, and I'm your roommate. What did you do, resign?"

"Yes, I resigned! I resigned a little over an hour ago, in front of a press conference, in Jeb Maxwell's office."

"Why would you want to do a thing like that?"

"I explained all that at the press conference."

"Good for you. Except nobody saw it."

"*Everybody* saw it! People are stopping me on the street congratulating me on it."

"My God. You really don't know, do you?"

"Of course, I know! I'm not senile, at least not yet! I know what I said in my own speech!"

Laurencia smiled, and said:

"Which speech?"

"The one I've been talking about! In heavens name, are we doing 'Who's on First' here? I feel like Lou Costello! There's only one speech! The one I resigned in!"

A shake of the head:

Then:

"That was your first speech of the day, my dear. The one people are talking about is your second."

"My..."

"Yes, your Second Inaugural Address, as it were."

And then, finally, Nina began to understand.

"You mean, in my office..."

"That's what I mean."

"But that was just for my staff!"

"No. It was for your staff, and their iPhones."

"Someone taped it?"

"They all taped it."

"That's impossible! I would have seen it!"

"Did you ever see it when you were teaching?"

"No, but..."

"See? You're talking about the youth of today."

"But...but...you mean, someone made a recording of me...and then sent the recording somewhere?"

Another shake of the head.

The chicken was fast disappearing now.

"Nina, Nina, Nina. Try to understand this: THEY ALL WERE FILMING YOU AS YOU WERE TALKING! And as soon as you finished, they were all Facebooking their friends, and LIKES started pouring in from around the country and then you were being Twittered and then you were being YouTubed and now you're the hottest thing since this chicken used to be when it still existed."

It took Nina some moments to begin to comprehend all of this.

Finally, she whispered:

"I'm viral. I've gone viral."

"You have done that, baby."

"And what I told the staffers is all around the country?"

"Naw, silly, it's all around the world!"

"This is incredible."

"It's happening, though."

"Laurencia, what shall I do? I can't even go back to our apartment. Oh, and for God's sakes, I have to apologize to you!"

"For what?"

"For getting you involved in this! Your lovely apartment—it's all surrounded by reporters!"

"Don't be ridiculous! This is all great fun—the most I've had in years! Except for the part about you resigning. You can't resign, you know."

"But I did resign!"

"Well then, we shall have to get together and un-resign you."

"Who?"

"I and a few *Sisters* on the hill. We're all a part of the Black Caucus."

"The Black Caucus is going to be defending me?"

"The female part of the Black Caucus. We call ourselves the Black Women's Caucus."

"I didn't know there even was a Black Women's Caucus."

Laurencia smiled.

"Everywhere there are black women, baby, there are *Black Women's Caucuses*. There have to be, because black men are dogs."

"I thought men were pigs."

"Cultural difference. White women think men are pigs. Black women think they're dogs."

"Maybe we should all come together and try to figure that out. It will be our first job when we take over power."

"I'm all for that."

"But there's still the question: what do I do now?"

"Stay here. I put a couple of books in the overnight bag. Nobody knows you're here. I'll sneak back over in a few hours and bring you dinner. Other than that, let's just see what develops."

She got up, walked to the doorway, opened it, looked back, and said, firmly:

"After I've gone, turn on the TV. You'll be surprised at what you see."

She waited a moment.

She retrieved the remote from its place on top of the television.

Then she returned to the bed, got under the covers, and turned the set on.

A TV anchorwoman was speaking:

"Hello, America; I'm Christine Richardson and this is *CNN in the Afternoon*! And what an afternoon it is proving to be! For it was only a few hours ago that a trim, soft-spoken Mississippi woman, a career schoolteacher, resigned from her position in the U.S. House of Representatives, a position she had only just attained in a courageous battle against all odds. But that was not all. She offered the resignation because she refused to yield to pressure from her party, and, CNN has just learned, pressure from her own president. Just five minutes later, she returned to her own office, called her staff together in a circle around her, and delivered the following speech:"

The quality of the video deteriorated slightly.

Not much though. Nina gave the photographer/recorder that much.

These iPhones.

There she was, little Nina Bannister, dressed in her *high school principal* beige suit.

She recognized her own words.

"Do you know why this entire mess has come about? Men. Only about a fourth of..."

Etc. Etc. Etc.

The whole speech.

Including, of course:

"And *they* are governing *us*? Why? Why are we allowing this? WE OUTNUMBER THEM! What is the matter with us?"

And on, until the end.

Nina barely recognized it, so outraged had she been while giving it.

And now, the whole country was hearing it.

Again, back to Christine Richardson.

"The effect of this speech, which began spreading on social media networks no more than fifteen seconds after it was given, has been shocking. The speech is everywhere. It's being talked about everywhere. And people are coming together. In city after city across this nation, *The Nina Speech*, as it has already been dubbed, is being played over loudspeakers fixed on vans making their way through the streets. Los Angeles, Philadelphia, Detroit—CNN's cameras are now live at a women's rally in downtown Milwaukee. We take you there now..."

Switch of scenes.

Huge group of women milling about, some shouting, some merely shaking their fists at the camera.

Another reporter:

"Ma'am?"

Angry middle-aged woman:

"Yes?"

"Can you tell me why you and these other protesters have come down here today?"

"Damned right, I can tell you! We're here because we're sick of things, the way they're going. This woman finally had the guts to say it like it is! We *do* outnumber the men! Why the hell are we letting them make all the decisions? They're pigs anyway!"

Black woman's face in front of the camera now.

"Dogs, honey!"

We are, thought Nina, *going to have to get this worked out among us.*

CHAPTER SIX: STUPID IS AS STUPID DOES

Next morning, the following front page article appeared in *The New York Times*:

FEMINIST DEMONSTRATIONS ROCK NATION
Special to *The New York Times*
By
Elizabeth Cohen

Beginning late yesterday afternoon and lasting well into the early morning hours today, sporadic demonstrations have been taking place in various cities around the United States. These events have differed dramatically in their size and format, but they have all centered around one common theme: the government is broken, and the people to fix it are women.

Catalyst for these demonstrations appears to be Congresswoman Nina Bannister, D-Mississippi, who resigned her post in the government yesterday at 3:15 p.m., immediately after answering *no* to a question by this reporter inquiring as to whether she actually believed an apology she had read minutes earlier. The *no*, in and of itself, may have been little noticed around the nation; but what certainly *was* noticed was an *ad hoc* speech that ex-Congresswoman Bannister delivered only minutes later to a tight circle of her own staff, and which was recorded as she gave it. She laced the news about her resignation with a stinging rebuke to her male counterparts, who, she cried out passionately, lacked the ability to compromise and work together for the common good of all people—an ability that women across the entire political spectrum seemed to possess.

Ex-Congresswoman Bannister then went on to point out that only one-fourth of US House and Senate members are women, an extraordinary statistic given the fact that a majority of all voters across the country are female. "WE OUTNUMBER THEM!" she could be seen and heard crying out. "WHAT IS THE MATTER WITH US?"

This speech began—shortly after its conclusion— appearing on computer screens and smart phones around the country. It spread like wildfire through all channels of social media, and by late afternoon had begun appearing on radio broadcasts and late afternoon television news channels. Its effect was shocking. It seemed to galvanize voters, especially women voters, who appeared to sympathize with the small, primly-dressed, ex-school teacher from a small coastal village in southern Mississippi.

"We love Nina!" signs appeared in the streets, along with pictures of the ex-congresswoman. Other signs and posters, hastily drawn in some instances, showed various depictions of the Greek heroine Lysistrata, title character of a play by the ancient comic writer Aristophanes, in which the women of Athens and Sparta agree to go on a sex strike until the ruinous Peloponnesian War is brought to a close by the men who have been waging it.

More than a thousand protesters took to the streets in Los Angeles, many of them women, many of them carrying banners saying, ostensibly to men, "IF YOU DON'T COME ACROSS, WE DON'T COME ACROSS!"

There are no final reports on precisely how many demonstrations have taken place so far, or how many are planned for later on today. Observers have commented, however, that nothing similar has taken place on such a wide scale around the nation, since Susan B. Anthony led suffragettes in a battle to give women the vote.

That battle was ended decades ago.

Women did, in fact, win the right to vote.

Now a similar battle is being waged to see if they can win the right to govern the nation.

ELIZABETH COHEN
NEW YORK TIMES

Three hours after the appearance of the article, at approximately nine a.m., a group of six women, five of them African American, one of them Caucasian, made their way into a conference room adjoining the offices of Jeb Maxwell, House Minority Whip.

The Caucasian woman was ex-Congresswoman Nina Bannister.

The five African American women were members of the Black Women's Caucus, an organization that did not officially exist but had been called into being on an informal basis several years previously, due to the fact that, as was stated by one of its members (name not known), *men are dogs*.

The African American women were dressed more colorfully than ex-Congresswoman Bannister, who wore only a beige suit and no hat.

The hats surrounding her, on the other hand, were broad-brimmed, feathered, and set at striking angles.

As were the scarves, neckties, purses, and other accessories.

It took some moments for all of these Senators and Representatives (for the caucus spanned both legislative bodies) to be seated, coffeed, and introduced (something that was done only for the record, since the House Whip knew all of them).

These formalities being attended to, Jeb Maxwell, seated at the end of the oaken table, began the meeting:

"I'm so happy that you asked to come and have this chat."

(This was a lie, of course, since the House Whip was terrified of the meeting, and had been since he had been *invited* to have it at nine the previous evening, as the result of a telephone call placed to his home by Laurencia Dalrymple, who everybody on Capitol Hill feared much more than the president, whom nobody very much feared.)

(Nor had anybody come into the conference room to *chat*, but that was a word that had come into common parlance among people of great power and mutual disrespect, and served to betoken, much like the word *folks*, that we were all just good common country people sitting out on our porches and swapping tales, much as had been done in simpler better times.)

"And I also want to say, Congresswoman Bannister…"

"Actually, Congressman Maxwell…"

Senator Dalrymple used the word *Congressman* much as a general might have used the word *private*....

"…Actually, the correct term should probably be ex-Congresswoman. You do realize that our friend Nina offered her resignation yesterday from the United States House of Representatives."

"Yes, yes, of course I realize that. But I'm hoping that it's something we can get straightened out."

"Straightened out? Why? Is it crooked?"

Ha ha ha!

Ha ha ha!

Everyone sipped coffee.

The *chat* went on.

Among the *folks*.

"No, no, it's just that things got out of hand so quickly at the press conference. I had no idea, no idea at all, that you, Nina, objected to the statement you had just read to the press."

Laurencia Dalrymple:

"Really?"

"No!"

"Even though you had written it for her?"

"We simply thought it might be easier for her if we did that."

"And even though it contradicted what she had previously said concerning the children at the border?"

Deep breath by the Whip.

"I had merely tried to point out to Congress...ex-Congress..."

(This was proving to be quite a problem for the Whip.)

"...that the statement, so constituted as she gave it, did not comply with the party's position on this particular issue."

"Ah. And in pointing that out, you had occasion to call her stupid?"

Silence in the room.

Nina Bannister stared at Jeb Maxwell.

She was joined in doing this by five other faces, none of them smiling.

The Minority Whip, who was definitely in the minority now, and who was definitely being whipped, could only stare down at the table in front of him.

He must have felt, thought Nina, *much as she had felt the day previous, when she had been made to feel like a child being punished.*

"I...I regret that so deeply..."

"We all do, Mr. Congressman. You see, we—my *Sisters* and I—make it a point to treat each other with respect. We ask that our colleagues do the same."

"Of course, of course! It's just that we were all so taken aback by the comments…"

"And what, may we ask, about the comments so took you aback?"

"Well, only that…"

"Only that three hundred million Americans should feel ashamed of themselves watching children die in the desert while we do nothing to help them?"

"No, no, of course, we are, as you know, trying everything we can to help them."

"Are we?"

"Yes, we definitely are! It's just that, given the Republicans' unwillingness to aid in passing the president's…"

"So the Republicans are stupid too, I assume."

"Again, I am so sorry for the tone I must have seemed to adopt."

"Seemed?"

"Yes, surely…"

Laurencia Dalrymple merely smiled at Nina and said:

"What was it, my sister, that Prince Hamlet said?"

Nina knew this, of course, and had taught it thousands of times, and so could smile and say in response:

"Seems, Madame! Nay, it is; I know not seems."

A pause for a time.

Nods around the table.

A voice saying quietly:

"I know *that's* right!"

Another pause.

Then Laurencia Dalrymple:

"Congressman Maxwell, my fellow legislators and I, who have come to you today—and by the way, we *do* appreciate your agreeing to see us—"

"Of course, of course!"

"—but we also need you to realize one extremely important point. And that point is simply this: namely that yesterday morning, when Nina looked out across that group of reporters and said '*No*'—at that point, she became one of us."

"I understand."

"No, you don't. Because you've not had to say '*No*' as much as we have. But when we as *black women* hear the word *no* we take that very seriously."

To this, the Whip, barred from understanding, had nothing left to do but nod.

And after a time, Laurencia Dalrymple, satisfied that little Jeb Maxwell would get into no more fights on the playground or throw no more stones at the windows of the sixth grade classroom, eased up on him a little and even thought about giving him a candy bar which she had hidden in her desk drawer.

She spoke, though, to Nina.

"Nina, you realize the effect that your talk with your staff yesterday is having around the country?"

To this, Nina could only shake her head and say, quietly:

"I don't think I really do."

"You read *The New York Times* this morning?"

"Yes, I did."

"Well, honey, that story only gives you a hint of what's happening."

Jeb Maxwell leaned forward on the desk as Laurencia continued:

"It's the tip of the iceberg. Stories are coming in from everywhere. Everybody on Capitol Hill is being deluged with letters. 'Support our Nina!' And 'Nominate more women!' And 'Time for a sex change in November!'"

Nina shook her head:

"This is stunning. I don't know what to say."

To which Laurencia Dalrymple smiled.

Everyone, Nina now noticed, in the room was smiling.

"Nina, dear, I think the most important thing for you to say, if you will, is that you take back your resignation."

'I…I just…"

"We need you."

For a time, she could not speak.

Then she nodded, and in a voice that would have quavered had it been required to say more than two words, said two words:

"All right."

And Nina Bannister was back in Congress.

INTERLUDE

He had gotten used, by now, to the place he lived in.

The scuffling of feet on the sidewalk outside the window no longer bothered him.

He knew what he had to do.

A voice told him what he had to do, and he knew that voice to be God's.

So now he unwrapped the package that he had placed on the bed, carefully put the paper away, opened the long box, and stared down at the black oily surface of the rifle.

He took its scope carefully between his right thumb and forefinger.

And memories came flooding back to him.

Memories of his father, all those years ago, all those decades ago.

His father teaching him to hunt deer.

Memories of them walking stealthily through the deep woods of Mississippi and then sitting ever so quietly in the deer stand, aware of every small movement around them, waiting for the sun to set, moving not a muscle.

The voice came softly to him and invaded his memory.

SHE IS DETESTABLE. SHE IS TURNING RIGHTEOUSNESS INSIDE OUT.

SHE MUST BE DESTROYED.

Then it went away, and the memory could resume.

And, in it, a buck came slowly out of the undergrowth, raised its massively horned head, sniffed the air around it, lowered its head, and began to eat.

He could remember taking aim ever so carefully, squeezing the trigger, and exulting as he heard the bullet *splat* against the animal's side.

CHAPTER SEVEN: OLD DEAD GREEKS

At 5:30 that same evening, Nina found herself entering the station headquarters of WRV Washington, there to be interviewed by a woman named Danielle Slaughter, who was the anchor of *The Capitol Dome*, the city's highest-rated evening news program.

She seemed to find herself facing a good many professional women with microphones in their hands, and so this one, she felt, was beginning "to fade into the light of common day."

As Wordsworth might have described the phenomenon of all anchor women beginning to resemble each other.

This woman was not as tall as the reporter who had interviewed her two hours earlier, but then that reporter was taller than any woman Nina had been interviewed by except for Liz Cohen.

She was not as serious as the woman from Vicksburg, who had done the interview that had gotten her in trouble, but she did not have the chatty, constant, glowing brisk smile as the woman from the Bay St. Lucy paper who had interviewed her on the morning following her election to the House of Representatives.

No, the only thing that stood out about this woman was the fact that she made Nina worry by telling her so often not to worry.

"Just be yourself, and everything will go fine."

"Okay. I can do that."

It was a bit awkward being told this while she was sitting in a chair like a barber's chair having makeup applied to her—*much too heavily*, she told herself.

"I guess the main thing is, just don't worry."

"I won't worry."

She began to worry.

Eyeliner going on now.

She never wore eyeliner.

Why did she need eyeliner?

"So have you been keeping up with the last hours around the country?"

"Not really. I had to take a car over here, and I went by the office—the mail is amazing."

"No, what's amazing are the demonstrations. There's one planned tonight here in the city. Will you go?"

"I don't know. I just..."

Someone sticking a head in the makeup room door:

"Two minutes, Ms. Slaughter."

"Right."

Door closing.

Ms. Slaughter to Nina:

"You're not worried now, are you?"

"No. I promise I'm not worried."

"Good. Because I'm just going to ask you some basic questions. The first question will be 'How have you been holding up under the strain of the last two days?' Got that?"

"I got it."

"It's always been my philosophy that people being interviewed worry less if they know what the first question is going to be."

"That makes sense."

"So again—your first question will be 'How have you been holding up under the strain of the last two days?'"

"I understand."

"And you're not worried?"

"Not a bit."

She could now feel sweat forming in her armpits.

"Ms. Slaughter?"

"Yes?"

"Time!"

"All right, Nina. Follow me. Right through here!"

And so she was led out to face the cameras.

National TV.

National TV!

She was put into a chair, with Danielle Slaughter facing her, smiling.

Shadowy figures sat behind desks stretching back into a room surrounding her.

There was music playing now.

People were gesturing to each other, whispering.

The music got louder.

She was now *really* worried.

Well. At least she knew the first question:

"How have you been holding up under the strain of the last two days?"

"Okay everybody, we're...we're...LIVE AND ON THE AIR!"

Huge smile at the camera from Danielle Slaughter.

Then:

"Good evening, Washington! I'm Danielle Slaughter and we're live from Capitol Hill. My guest tonight? Who else could it be? The lady whose face is popping up around the nation, and who seems to have instigated, almost single-womanly, the biggest potential electoral revolution since—well, since the Revolution! And so, without further ado, I give you Congresswoman Nina Bannister from the great state of Mississippi! Nina, welcome to the show!"

"Thank you!"

"The first question I have to ask you is: what was the Peloponnesian War, and who was Lysistrata?"

Nina stared at her:

"I'm sorry…"

What the hell happened to "How have you been bearing up under the strain?"

"Yes, if you could just tell us, what was the Peloponnesian War and who was Lysistrata?"

Nina took a deep breath, said to herself, *I'm bearing up quite well under the strain, and…*

"The Peloponnesian War was a terrible conflict fought between the Greek city state of Athens and a group of other city states under the leadership of Sparta. It lasted from 431 to 404 BC, and we know a great deal about it from the writings of the historian Thucydides. Sparta was essentially a land power, Athens a sea power, so they had a hard time getting at each other. Finally though, Athens conceived, in 413, a plan of an attack against Syracuse, a Spartan ally. The attack was a disastrous failure. Anybody in Athens should have been able to read the writing on the wall, but the war party was too strong, and the Athenians too proud. They had gotten so wrapped up in being a city state that they had forgotten what it meant to be Greece, to be a nation working together."

"And Lysistrata?"

"*Lysistrata* was a play written and performed just after the disaster at Syracuse. The writer was Aristophanes, who is known for creating Old Comedy. Old comedy is wild, crazy, unthinkable, and hilarious. Lysistrata, the title character, is herself an Athenian woman who gets all of the women in Athens to join with all the women in Sparta and demand that the war be ended—or else. The *or else,* of course, is a sex strike. They all plan to sequester themselves in the major buildings of the cities involved, and not give in to their husbands' desires until the fighting is stopped."

"Did it work, Nina?"

To which Nina could only shake her head.

"The play worked as a play and it's still done today. It's hilarious. But it didn't solve the war. The war ended with the complete destruction of Athens, and the severe weakening of Sparta. Greece as a whole never really recovered. The nation was conquered by Phillip of Macedon in 338 BC."

"And so, Nina, that leads to the big question. Given the unbelievable amount of support your impassioned speech has generated around the country, do you believe that the women of the United States should actually go on a sex strike?"

And it happened once again.

Those two categories of answers presented themselves clearly and unmistakably in her mind:

CORRECT ANSWER:

Danielle, I think that might be taking things a bit too far, and, of course, I never meant that women should stop having sex with their husbands. Nor, I'm sure, did Aristophanes. But sometimes a little shock is needed, and that's the role satire performs. I honestly do believe that certain things are true beyond question. It is beyond question that our government seems stuck in neutral. Each political party has staked out solid positions on vital areas of dispute, and neither seems willing to budge. It's a matter of pride, just as it was to the Athenians and Spartans. Also, it's beyond question that only approximately one-fourth of our legislators are women, even though women form the majority of the electorate. That seems insane to me. Finally, I do honestly believe that women are better listeners than men. They are more adept at compromising. They have strong beliefs, certainly, but they are in general more willing than men to at least modify these beliefs so that a common ground can be reached, and so that genuine problems can be solved before they become crises. So, should all women around the country go on a sex strike on, say, July 4? No, of course not, that would be ludicrous. But—should we think seriously about increasing women's role in the government in November? Yes. Definitely."

And that was the answer that she should have given to the question, 'Nina, do you actually believe that the women of the United States should go on a sex strike?"

As opposed to THE INCORRECT ANSWER, (which she actually gave) which was:

"Yes. On July 4th."

Every light in the studio seemed to get brighter.

CHAPTER EIGHT: HERE COME THE LISSIES!

Nina went back to her apartment, lay down, and took a nap.

She was still a bit groggy when her cell phone buzzed.

Only two people that she knew of had her number. One was Jackson Bennett; the other Laurencia Dalrymple.

She had nothing against talking with either of them.

So she flipped open the phone.

"Nina?"

"Laurencia!"

"Nina, we all watched the interview together. You were superb!"

"I should have been more tactful, shouldn't I?"

"Are you joking? We were all sitting around the room waiting for just such an answer. And when you said 'July 4,' why we all got out our calendars and circled the date. Some of the Sisters even got on the phones to their husbands and said, 'Honey, you got a new night to go bowling!'"

Nina mused for a time about the national benefits that would follow a sudden increase in bowling revenue, but was interrupted when Laurencia asked:

"Now are you going to the rally tonight?"

"I'm not sure. Will there really be ten thousand people there?"

"At least, baby. It's the coming out of the Lissies! And I'm going to be the featured speaker!"

"Who in God's name are the Lissies?"

Pause.

"You really don't know?"

"I feel like I'm the only one who doesn't know."

"That may be true. But come to the rally, baby. Disguise yourself so you won't be mobbed—but come to the rally!"

It could be said that the Mall—the heart of almost every visitor's trip to Washington—has influenced life in the U.S. more than any other expanse of lawn. On the Mall one can:

Ride an old fashioned carousel in front of the Smithsonian Castle

Watch the fireworks on the Fourth of July.

See the original Spirit of St. Louis.

Look at Dorothy's ruby slippers or Abraham Lincoln's top hat at the American History Museum.

Twirl around the ice skating rink in the National Gallery of Art's sculpture garden.

Or…

Exercise your first amendment rights by joining a rally or protest.

And this was, in fact, what Nina Bannister had decided to do.

It was insane, and she knew it.

But she could not stay away. Ten thousand people were to be gathering around the Washington Monument because of a movement that she herself had started little more than one day earlier. Her newest and quite possibly best friend Laurencia Dalrymple was to be addressing the crowd. This was to be the unveiling of the Lissies, an organization which, apparently, was attempting to stage a revolution in American politics.

And what in God's name *were* the Lissies?

So she decided to risk it.

At five thirty, she put on an old pair of ragged blue jeans, a sweatshirt (too heavy for this hot sultry weather but it gave her an illusion of being hidden), a thick pair of sunglasses and a floppy fishing hat that she had bought in a Dollar Store on her way back to the hotel.

She was so common and featureless as to be next to invisible.

And, so disguised, she strode out toward the Mall.

It was a twenty minute walk under a spectacularly clear sky, which was glowing golden in the sunset.

The crowd increased around her as she walked, and she could not help feeling excitement when she told herself again and again that this was actually true, was really happening, and had been started by her.

Then she began to be aware of the shirts.

Black, short-sleeved shirts with raised fists in white on either side of the silhouette of a woman.

The woman had a classic nose. Long curly hair flowed behind her neck.

Beneath these symbols was written the word—

LISSIE!

And then she realized.

"Oh, my God."

Lissie was short for Lysistrata.

The Lissies had formed their own movement. And their color was not pink.

It was black.

And its symbol included a pair of upraised fists.

Clearly the Lissies were not to be dabbled with.

The crowd became more dense as she approached the monument, which was bathed in white light.

It was a strange crowd. It reminded her somewhat of the group of environmentalists who had taken over the beach in Bay St. Lucy following Liz Cohen's story revealing the alleged malfeasance on board Aquatica. But it was different, too. There was the obligatory marijuana, of course; but there were long patches of earth and air where nothing was being smoked at all. There were young women in bandannas wearing hooped earrings and tie-dyed shirts; but there were middle-aged women who looked like they belonged in the local Parent Teacher Association of Bay St. Lucy.

There was music everywhere, of course.

But it was music of every sort. Rock music, folk music, Bluegrass music…

…and most of it coming from female ensembles.

Also everywhere were signs.

Professionally painted signs, slapped together signs, small signs, big signs…

…and a few signs with her own picture on them, above the words:

"NINA FOR PRESIDENT!"

What had she started?

Policemen were around her now, channeling the stream of people who were moving like a jubilant river—for all of these people seemed happy, as though they were being drawn toward a gigantic Christmas tree where a completely unexpected present awaited them.

The crowd was not, she found herself realizing, all female. Just as there were women of all ages and dresses and hairstyles and heights and weights and ethnicities and religions and pet ownerships (Dogs predominated, but other animals appeared here or there and one woman had a python draped around her neck)—just as there were all of these varieties of femaledom, so was there an equal diversity of men.

One of whom, a slender professorial type with a silver beard, carried a sign saying:

WE GIVE UP. TAKE OVER!

More signs proliferated now, as though the very banners and images were preparing in advance for a prolonged sex strike by taking matters into their own hands and reproducing.

GAYS AND LESBIANS FOR LISSIE!

ON JULY 4—NO NO NO NO!

TRANSGENDER AMERICA FOR NINA!

MEN MAKE WARS! WOMEN MAKE BABIES!

MEN: THE EARTH'S TESTOSTERONLY ENEMY!

HISPANIC WOMEN SAY 'BRING IN THE CHILDREN!'

MEN: LEARN TO COOK!

There were people everywhere, all of them speaking in excited tones, all of them pointing at the signs, the signs, the signs—and the fireworks arrays that now were blossoming across the darkening sky above the Potomac.

"Look at that group!"

"Look at him!"

"Look at her!"

"What do those tattoos say?"

"What kind of an animal is that, a monitor lizard?"

"I've never seen a protest mounted this fast!"

"But it's not really a protest, is it?"

No, Nina found herself thinking. *No, it's a baby shower.*

Welcome to earth, all the new born Lissies.

Finally, she had drifted half a mile or more in the surge of humanity that surrounded her, and she found herself in sight of the stage. There were musicians on it, of course, as there must have been on any stage gawked at by so many clapping and shouting and stomping people.

The wail of electrified guitars sifted through the balmy, cherry-blossomed, late spring air.

She was aware for the first time of the moon—full, pale, but growing darker yellow by the moment—and grinning down on the festivities, seemingly unconcerned that the Man in the Moon might soon be replaced by the Woman in the Moon, who could do the satellite's job more efficiently.

Policemen and women mounted astride huge reddish-brown horses strode patiently beside them as they flowed along, the officers halting occasionally beside smaller groups who were shouting at each other and waving fists in the air.

For this, disagreement, too, was a part of what went on in the Mall.

First Amendmenters having at each other.

"Women belong at home!"

"*You* belong at home!"

A group of young, tattooed women:

"WE'RE GLAD WE'RE GAY!"

A group of young, tattooed men:

"WE'RE GLAD YOU'RE GAY TOO!"

Two middle-aged women in bonnets and aprons, holding bibles aloft:

"Wives, obey your husbands! Wives, obey your husbands!"

Which elicited the reply, from somewhere in the crowd:

"Husbands, honor your wives. And *vote* for them!"

A husky, bearded man, who was making a trumpet by cupping his hands over his mouth:

"The man is the head of the house!"

Replied to by a husky, non-bearded woman who did not need to make a trumpet because nothing was over her mouth:

"Then get the hell back in the house!"

Officers staring hard at both of them, horses standing placidly between shouters.

They moved on.

The rock band was leaving the stage, and Nina could see a line of colorfully dressed people stepping up onto it.

The Washington Monument was precisely behind the stage; its tip almost touched the bottom of the circle that was the moon.

More signs, some of them actually offering information:

I THINK CONGRESS IS DOING A GOOD JOB: 31%

I THINK CONGRESS IS DOING A POOR JOB: 60%

I DON'T CARE: 9%

AP POLL, YESTERDAY.

But most of them simply confrontational, such as the one being waved by a group of men wearing cowboy hats and plaid shirts:

GOD IS A MAN!

Which was, of course, responded to by a group of young women, who had just made their own sign, and printed it in black marker:

SO *THAT'S* WHY THINGS ARE SO SCREWED UP!

And on and on.

Until, finally, the group of people on the stage took their seats.

A tall woman dressed in a navy suit and wearing a gold scarf came to the microphone.

The microphone squealed out across the crowd, which seemed vast to Nina.

She surveyed it, spread out behind her, moving restlessly, chanting and gesturing and laughing and cursing and drinking and attempting, completely unsuccessfully because of the density of the group, to play Frisbee.

"My fellow Americans..."

Squeal squeal squeal…

Settle down crowd, settle down crowd…

"My fellow Americans, my name is Cynthia Dodsworthy, and I am the junior senator from Oregon."

Cheers.

Clapping.

Boos.

Shouting.

Dogs howling.

From somewhere, a roman candle shooting upward, exploding, then fading out into a dozen or so smoking snake trails across the now purple sky.

"I have the honor of introducing tonight's featured speaker."

"A proper introduction for her, on any normal occasion, might take several minutes, or even longer. But this is hardly a normal occasion. And so, I'm simply going to ask her to come up here. Ladies and gentlemen, Senator Laurencia Dalrymple!"

Wild cheering.

And Laurencia, dressed all in red and wearing an African print scarf, unprepossessing, hardly tall or statuesque…

…but standing behind a wonderful smile and peering out over an adoring audience…

Laurencia spoke into the microphone, which, awed by her, quieted down immediately.

Everyone quieted down.

It was as though a good principal—and Nina knew this because she had been a good principal—had stepped into the center of the crowded gym floor before third period and stood there, arms folded, saying soundlessly:

"Be quiet. Now."

And so where there had been barking and yowling and arguing and screaming and cursing and flirting and airplane-droning and Frostie wagon jingling and humanity howling...

...there was now only the scarcely perceptible fall of cherry blossom pollen.

So that Laurencia could begin.

"We are all gathered here, *Sisters* and *Brothers*, on this extraordinary night, because one woman, yesterday afternoon, had the courage to say *no*."

Thousand one thousand two...

Wild cheering.

The moon broadened its smile and, at least some observers swear, rocked back and forth slightly in its hole in the sky.

After a few years silence again covered the crowd.

"And with that *no*,' the Lissie Movement officially began!"

More wild cheering.

The moon remained stationary, having come to its senses and recognized the impropriety of its previous movement.

Silence having returned...

"What an extraordinary twenty four hours! Have there been a similar twenty-four hours in the history of this great city, of this splendid Mall on which we find ourselves assembled? Have there been? Ever?"

"NO! NO! NO! NO!"

And Laurencia, shaking her head, playing the emotion, working the crowd:

"NO NO NO, I agree and I agree and I agree and who could NOT agree? Who could look out across this field of Lissiedom and NOT agree? No one! And so, my gentle Sisters and Brothers, it remains for me now to admit my tardiness. Yes, yes, many of you were here before me. But I have arrived. And I know what I must do, this very moment!"

So saying, in one infinitely graceful and sweeping gesture, she removed her red suit coat, removed her scarf, reached into a cardboard box that had sat unnoticed behind her...

...then took out a black Lissie t-shirt and put it on over her white blouse.

And somewhere a brass band started playing.

Nina looked around; she could not see it.

But what could she see, in this vast and milling sea of people?

The band must have been set up half a mile away.

But someone in the Lissie Party understood acoustics.

For here came the trumpets and the trombones.

The melody: "It'll be a hot time in the old town tonight!"

CHEER CHEER CHEER

FOR THE WOMAN OF THE YEAR!

I TELL YOU...

CHEER CHEER CHEER

FOR THE WOMAN OF THE YEAR!

And so on and so on.

For at least a minute.

Laurencia, arms straight above her head, shouting and dancing and grinning and pointing at the shirt, and at the silhouette of Lysistrata.

Finally, the song died down; Laurencia got her breath, and continued:

"I will tell you the truth. I do not know where Nina Bannister is right now..."

She's right here, thought Nina.

"...but in a larger sense, I do know. She is here, just as sure as all of us are here."

Okay, thought Nina, *so maybe I was right after all.*

"Her spirit fills all of us, and her *no* rings continually in our ears."

Cheering.

Stop cheering!

Cheering stopped.

"But the beautiful thing is, that *no* has turned into a *yes*. That *no* has been what our senators and representatives have been saying to each other for the last year, the last years, the last decades—with the result that we now have a paralyzed government, incapable of compromise, and thus incapable of basic humanity!"

"I know *that's* right!"

"Yes!"

"Tell 'em!"

"You tell em about it!"

"Uhh huh! Uhh huh!"

"That's my Sister! That's my Sister!"

"But the *yes* it's turned into—and in the wink of an eye, so incredibly fast does it seem—is the Lissie Movement!"

Band.

CHEER CHEER CHEER

FOR THE WOMAN OF THE YEAR!

…for another chorus or so.

Now the principal again.

Hands in the air.

Quieten down, students.

Or nobody goes to lunch.

"Now, there has been some confusion concerning what the Lissie Movement actually is, and what it hopes to accomplish. Since Lissies have only existed for a little more than twenty-four hours, that may be understandable."

General laughter.

"But perhaps now I can clarify. First, The Lissie Movement cannot, at this stage of the election cycle, hope to become a legitimate third party. All of us who are Republicans or Democrats or Unitarians should remain so and be proud of the fact. But what the Lissie Movement is, is a social action that has at its heart and soul one basic idea, one basic goal: namely that women should begin to play a larger role in the running of this great country, and they do so beginning this November!"

"Yes!"

"YES!"

"LISSIE FOREVER!"

"We have an entire summer in front of us as well as September and October. Seventeen senate seats are contested; but one hundred and sixty-nine seats are up for grabs. One hundred and sixty-nine. And, my brothers and sisters, even though each party may have chosen tentative candidates for those seats by now—NOTHING IS IN STONE! There is no legal reason why, given campaigns run with energy and strength and intelligence and passion—a hundred new women cannot be elected to Congress this very November. Yes. Yes, it could happen!"

"Tell em!"

"Tell em more!"

"Now, there is this little matter of July 4."

General laughter.

"And I know that it might be worrying some of you women. Newlyweds especially. The rest probably don't care any more."

"That's right!"

"You tell em!"

"They're dogs! All men are dogs!"

"They're pigs! All men are pigs!"

Why, Nina asked herself again, *can't we get this thing straight between us?*

"Well, I'm going to go on record now as stating that I am not in favor of a sex strike, and I don't see why we have to have one."

Stunned silence.

A few voices:

"We want the strike!"

"WE WANT THE STRIKE!"

"LET THE DOGS/PIGS (approximately equal numbers of each animal being shouted out) GO WITHOUT!"

But Laurencia Dalrymple simply smiled and said:

"I don't see why we have to have one at all. As I say, we're trying to elect one hundred new women to congress this November. Now, if by July 4, let's say, forty have been placed on ballots around the country—why, we don't have a problem. Let's all take those men to bed and show them a good time!"

Wild laughter at this.

"But…"

More voices.

"Uhhh huh!"

"Uhhh huh!"

"*Now* I hear you! *Now* I hear you!"

"But if we don't have that many women on the ballot. Well, I believe that in the play that Congresswoman Bannister was kind enough to teach us about, the women all came together in the Acropolis. And woe to any man who tried to get in there! We don't have an acropolis—but we have gymnasiums in every town in America!"

"Yes we do!"

"Yes we do!"

"And we don't need to call it a sex strike. That is so harsh, so vulgar. So we'll just give it a good name right now. As of right now, it is the July 4 Slumber Party sponsored by the Worldwide Movement of Lissie International!"

Wild cheering.

I can't believe this is happening, thought Nina.

What else can happen?

She was wondering what else could happen, when it did.

Laurencia continued:

"When Dr. King wrote his *Letter from a Birmingham Jail,* he ended it by saying, 'I can't believe I have written so long a letter.' Now the reason Dr. King wrote 'so long a letter,' as you all know, is that he was in jail."

Some laughter.

Quiet laughter.

Then:

"And I feel as though I have made 'so long a speech.' So I must end it. There is just one thing I want to announce, though, before we all disperse to go about our revolutionary—and my Sisters and Brothers, I honestly do feel it to be revolutionary—work. And that thing I want to announce is this: I do hereby declare my candidacy for the Presidency of the United States."

CHAPTER NINE: BEWARE OF GREEK SHIPS BEARING WOMEN

On the morning of May 8, one week after Laurencia Dalrymple's announcement of her candidacy for presidency and slightly less than two months before the termination of sex in the United States of America by order of Nina Bannister, Nina herself received a letter from Helen Reddington.

She was able to read it sitting in the kitchen of the apartment she shared with Senator Dalrymple, since ample security measures had been set up to guarantee a modicum of privacy for the two women living there.

The letter read as follows:

Dear Nina,

Congratulations on everything you've been doing! Bay St. Lucy is ecstatic and proud. At least the women are. The men walk around looking kind of stunned.

I know you've got a million things to do, Nina, and Jackson tells us that you've probably also got a million letters to read and answer. So I'll make this brief.

We have an idea. Actually, it was John who suggested it, but when I heard it, I knew his instincts were right on.

You remember the horrible *Hamlet* that turned out so disastrously. I'm sure you couldn't forget it, and I never will. That time spent under domination from Clifton; the slaps, the verbal abuse, the beatings—and, of course, the horrible way he died.

No, I'll never completely get over that, as happy as I now am with John and the animals.

The idea, though, Nina—the idea of the play itself, and having it done at the Auberge des Arts here in Bay St. Lucy—that idea was valid.

The one performance we actually got to give was a good one. The idea of using the roof of the Auberge as the battlements, and having Hamlet peer out over the gulf as though it were the North Sea. That all worked, and we produced a great tragedy, if even a greater tragedy hadn't overshadowed it.

So, why don't we mount another production?

I've already talked to people in New York. Given the publicity you've stirred up, they're wild about it.

We'll do it on the Fourth of July. The July 4 Slumber Party sponsored by the Worldwide Movement of Lissie International!"

Except, Nina, we won't do *Hamlet*.

The New York Shakespeare Company does other classical works, you know.

Sometimes they do Greek tragedies.

Sometimes they even do Greek comedies.

This time they need to do *Lysistrata*.

And I need to play the lead.

I've just finished reading the play for the first time, Nina. I'm ashamed that it's taken me this long. But it's a fantastic play! It's hilarious! The scene when the horny woman tries to get out of the Acropolis, saying that she's pregnant—and they whap on her big stomach and find out there's a soldier's metal helmet under her dress!

I can be Lysistrata, Nina, I know I can.

Like I say, I've already talked with a number of New York production people I know. The ideas are flying back and forth like wildfire. And there's money. Bay St. Lucy's rich, you know that. Big oil is still behind you, and their CEO still loves you—she's a feminist at heart.

The Company itself is willing to invest and invest big time. Lissie Day—which is what the Fourth is being called now for short—is *your* day, and you are centered in Bay St. Lucy. So—remember the play's first scene, in which the Spartan women, muscular old Lampito leading them, comes into Athens to meet with the Athenian women and Lysistrata? Well, we'll add a bit to the script and have them sail across the Saronic Gulf and land at Piraeus, which is only a few miles from Athens.

They could have actually done this!

Of course, we'll hire the Gulf of Mexico to play the Saronic Gulf.

Water is water, right?

And if our Gulf could play the North Sea—but it gets better!

There's a shipbuilding club in Boston that wants to take part. They claim to be able to construct for us a vessel that looks exactly like one the Spartans might have used.

We'll meet the Spartan women right down there on the beach in front of the Auberge des Arts!

And get this: at the end of the play, all the choruses unite and dance together, celebrating the end of the war. We'll switch the ending, though. At the end of our play, Lysistrata will announce from the rooftop of the Auberge whether forty new women have been put on ballots nationwide for the November elections. If the answer is *yes*, then the whole community, audience and all, will dance, sing, and basically get ready to have an orgy.

If *no*—then the women of Bay St. Lucy head for the gym.

Along with women all over the country.

Every major TV station will be carrying this thing, Nina!

What do you think?

Still your most adoring student,
Helen

It took Nina perhaps five minutes to read the letter.

After she did so, she walked into the study, took out her own letter writing paper, and wrote simply:

Helen,
I'm there.
Nina.

CHAPTER TEN: A NIGHT IN THE LIBRARY

Nina Bannister loved the library.

It was her second soul, so to speak.

She was thrust into the world of politics; not just politics in general but POLITICS FOR WOMEN!

And what did she know about the subject?

Women were ruling countries all over the world, and women were taking on major roles in running her own country.

What did these women have to say about their struggles, their difficulties, their defeats, their victories?

And so, the same night she had received news of Helen Reddington's *Lysistrata* production—which she found to be a superb idea—she took a cab to the Georgetown University Library. Having been told that, of course, she could access the catalogue and shelves, even as a visitor, as long as she checked nothing out. And having been shown, in answer to her inquiry concerning the quietest place to read, to a vacant carrel on the tenth floor (Spring semester had just ended, so there was a good deal of room in the library).

Having done all of these things, she made a glutton of herself on the contents of one of the nation's finest university libraries.

By eight o'clock, she had a paper cup of vending machine coffee in front of her (against library rules but she was all alone up here, so who was to care?)—and she was reading the publication blurb which appeared on the back cover of Dee Dee Myers' *Why Women Should Rule the World.*

The blurb read:

What Would Happen If Women Ruled the World?

"Everything could change, according to former White House Press Secretary Dee Dee Myers in her book *Why Women Should Rule the World*. Politics would be more collegial. Businesses would be more productive. And communities would be healthier. Empowering women would make the world a better place—not because women are the same as men—but precisely because they are different.

Blending memoir, social history, and a call to action, Dee Dee Myers challenges us to imagine a not-too-distant future in which increasing numbers of women reach the top ranks of politics, business, science, and academia. Reflecting on her own tenure in the Clinton administration and her work as a political analyst, media commentator, and former consultant to NBC's *The West Wing*, Myers assesses the crucial but long-ignored strengths that female leaders bring to the table. 'Women tend to be better communicators, better listeners, better at forming consensus,' Myers argues. 'In a highly competitive and increasingly fractious world, women possess the kind of critical problem-solving skills that are urgently needed to break down barriers, build understanding, and create the best conditions for peace.'"

My kind of woman, thought Nina.

And she plunged into the book.

By nine o'clock, she had finished it and felt like a prophet newly inspired.

Yes! Dee Dee was right, and *No!* Nina was not insane nor were the Lissies, nor was Laurencia Dalrymple!

Forty new people on national ballots.

Between now and November.

It could happen!

And if it did not...

...well, there would be a nation of men watching baseball games on television late into the night on July 4.

Thus inspired, she left her carrel unattended for a few minutes, got a second cup of coffee, left it steaming on the desk, and took a short bathroom break.

During this time, she had no idea that a figure had entered the carrel and dropped a tablet of some kind into the coffee.

So that everything looked precisely the same when she returned, opened *The Life of Anne Richards,* and took a sip.

Different taste?

Probably her imagination.

She was on page 23, when she went quietly asleep, her head on the desk.

The door to her carrel being closed, no one saw that she was there.

At midnight, the library closed.

She awoke at one a.m. to find herself alone on the deserted tenth floor.

There was a moment's panic.

How would she get out?

Then she realized that the doors leading to the stairwells all opened outward. There would be, at most, a bit of embarrassment if she should encounter a watchman stationed on the library's main floor.

Were there watchmen at one in the morning?

Were watchmen needed?

Were there roving gangs of thugs intent on breaking into the stacks in the wee hours, after nights of clubbing and binge drinking, intent on pillaging whatever they could find of fourteenth-century English literature?

The speculation gave her a smile as she got her things together, turned out the small reading light burning in the shelf above and just before her, and, unfolding like an accordion, forced her sleep-ridden knees to straighten.

She turned, exited the carrel, and peered through the austere and musty stacks.

Emergency lamps secreted high in corners emitted enough glimmering light so that she could see the elevators. They would not be running now, of course, but there were stairwells adjacent to them.

As she walked, she was just able to make out the titles of volumes surrounding her.

Piers Plowman

Annals of Fourteenth Century Literature

Second Edition, Chaucer, *Troilus and Cressida,*

Second Shepherd's Play, Critical Commentary.

She moved with a kind of reverence as though she had broken into a cathedral on All Saints Day and was in danger of disturbing the relics. She had just passed from the early to the late fifteenth century when she heard someone walking through the stacks immediately to her left—perhaps four or five rows over—taking down books, opening them, and laughing softly.

She could not have described that laughter. It was robbed of gaiety, spirit or energy. It was a dry laughter, the color of ready-to-burn leaves.

And it frightened her.

She had no idea why.

The fact that anyone would be here at this time of night was, of course, disturbing. But then, she herself was here. The figure shuffling along through centuries of English literature could have been an eccentric faculty member—almost certainly was a faculty member...immersed in another time, chuckling over forgotten verses and untranslatable colloquialisms.

Faculty members had carrels that were not alcoves, as hers was, but entire offices. Surely, it would not have been surprising to find a professor sitting at his office computer at one a.m. why would it be any different here?

Why was she frightened?

Dangerous people did not inhabit libraries.

She had almost convinced herself of that fact, and was on the point of identifying herself, when she heard a high cackling voice:

"I have been watching you."

Then absolute silence, followed by the tiniest of clicking sounds, metallic, clicking, opening and closing, opening and closing.

And...click...click...click...

Finally she realized:

It was a knife.

"I have been watching you. I have been told to watch you. And I have. You and the others. The others who follow you."

She could not move. She strained, almost against her own will, to see through the stacks, but there were too many of them. Nothing was visible except the implacable white-paneled ceiling above her, and, far to her right and left, windows that did not unlatch or move, opening out onto the campus with its rows of live oaks glowing in soft yellow street lamps.

"You are detestable. And your goals are detestable. All of them."

What was the next sound?

She could hear the book's pages being carefully cut out, one by one. Then there was a scratching sound.

"There is a Hell. And a devil in Hell. And, if you continue in these perverse ways..."

After a time, she could smell smoke.

He was burning the pages.

She could see the wisps of smoke rising above the stacks , whirling in ashen clouds as they made their way up through the circular ventilator in the middle of the ceiling.

"You will burn in Hell. Just as this paper is burning."

Then all sounds stopped.

The smoke continued to swirl in miniature rising funnel clouds, whirling aimlessly higher, drawn through the dust particles she could now see floating in what she had assumed, always, had been sterilized air.

Then she could hear footsteps moving toward the end of the fifth stack, a bit faster, shuffling, shuffling, until they reached the end of the row, and began making their way toward her.

She lifted her purse, slung it over one shoulder, and walked quickly to her left.

Whoever this was, she did not want to see him.

He had a knife, and he was ripping out and burning pages of books, at one in the morning, while telling her that she was detestable.

No, she needed to get out. And now.

It was as though she was in a canyon of literature, its walls towering above her, the river that had carved it having disappeared long ago, tile flooring all that remained of the fossilized creatures once inhabiting it.

Where was the break in the stacks?

There!

Turn there!

She did, breaking into an open area, a clearing, and there in front of her, the elevators.

The footsteps, purposeful now, were coming down the stack-row she had just left. She threw herself against the elevator and rammed the flat of her palm against the *down* button; it remained colorless, the elevators having been cut off.

From some fifteen feet behind her...for her back was to the shelves now... she heard a shout:

"Eve thou art dust! And to dust thou must return!"

And the footsteps continued, but with them, was interspersed the clicking sound.

Open shut open shut.

Click click click click.

Above her and just to her right glowed the white rectangle with red letters:

Exit.

The fire door, leading to the stairwell.

She threw herself against the rod that ran horizontally across it, precisely the height of her belt.

It gave with her weight; she lunged against it, and the heavy, army-gray door swung open, groaning slightly as it banged against the rail of an inner metal stairway leading downward.

She spun around and glanced backward. Through the foot-square glass window in the doorway she could see a figure emerge and come toward her.

She could also see that there was no way to lock the door from within the staircase.

She began to run down the stairs, grasping the rails at each landing, as she corkscrewed around tight turns leading flat across for three steps and then downward again...when, finding herself on the eighth level now...the tenth floor door burst open above her, a swampy green light bathing the well in which she found herself, and the singsong voice, not male or female, but seemingly mocking both genders in a kind of sexless cackle, erupted:

"You are hateful in the sight of God Almighty! And you will be put down and trodden upon, even as the serpent is trodden upon!"

She continued to descend, palms wet now and slipping on the pipes that were handrails.

The white-lighted floor number—6.

"Woman is an abomination!"

She could hear the rubber soles of her own sneakers squealing on the steps as she descended.

"BUT NOT UNSEEN BUT NOT UNSEEN! FOR GOD SEES ALL!"

Finally, she reached the main floor and burst through the doors, running now and trying not to hear the quick-shuffling footsteps behind her.

The check-out desk spread before her, computer screens glowing green on top of it, while a forest of dark similar screens surrounded her like square and blackened flowers sprouting from the tables used by undergraduates during the day, and only lines of impediment and useless demarcation in this ozone-buzzing half light.

Twenty steps and she was outside.

But did she want to go outside?

He could follow her there, too.

She stopped beside the reference desk and stared back at the doorway from which she had emerged, half expecting it to burst open, revealing…

…what?

What was this thing that was ripping books apart and setting fires in the library?

Nothing came from the door.

She could hear nothing, except, through the thick plate-glass windows far across the main floor, the mournful clanging of college cathedral bells.

No other sound.

What was he doing? Waiting behind the doors?

Or had he somehow found another entrance to the main floor?

She whirled, staring at the main entrance behind her.

Silent, black, empty...nothing at all moved or breathed in the vast ground floor of a library that could have been...and was, at least at this time of early morning...a cemetery for the thoughts of dead writers.

She should hide.

He was not watching her now, could not be.

She could hide in the restroom, there, just behind her.

But the restroom door could not be locked from the inside.

She would be vulnerable there, with no place to run.

Here, she might at least see him coming.

But outside?

Outside was better. She might be able to outrun him...thank God for the morning jogs, she was a good runner...

...and she was strong.

Let him try what he would try.

Also, outside there might, almost certainly would, be people. She could scream if need be. The campus was never truly deserted, and revelers always wandered from dorm to dorm or frat house to all night bar.

That decided, she would make for the main doors and go outside.

She had just taken the first steps in that direction when the alarms started going off.

First, red lights over the door in front of her; then similar lights hanging from the ceiling to her left.

Then there were red lights everywhere, and the piercing scream of bomb-warning sirens, or something similar:

EEEEEEEEEEE

Dentist drills magnified and sharpened, while the entire football field of chairs, desks, terminals, volumes, shelves, and founder-portraits flashed and shadowed, reddened and darkened—pulsated like a midway on Saturday night.

She looked back—still nothing coming out of the stairwell exit…

…but could she even see a figure if it did emerge, so surreal had the hall become.

EEEEEEEEEE

What the hell was going on?

A rattling behind her: she whirled toward the main entrance, where a figure was unlocking the glass double doors.

Rattle. Rattle.

EEEEEEEEEE

Finally, these doors burst open and a policeman entered.

She was standing now just beside the check out desk. She leaned over it, her lips only inches above hard black whatever material might have been its surface, and, now letting her forehead rest on the counter, she lisped out the words, "Thank you, thank you, thank you."

"What is going on here?"

The patrolman walked quickly toward her. He was an imposing figure, and might at any other time have been even more frightening than whatever kind of man/professor/lunatic/poetry reciter/book burner that had been following her.

"What is this? Ma'am, who are you? What is happening?"

He was a transformer, a creature from video games. There were arms, legs, badges, hair (for he carried his hat pinned between upper arm and chest) and even glasses…somehow it reassured her that he was wearing glasses…but enough additional paraphernalia hung off and extended outward from his blue trunk/torso as to render him a science-fiction cartoon. Gun, flashlight, key-ring, walkie-talkie…there was more of it than there was of him, and she remembered thinking, idiotically given the situation, that he was more hardware catalogue than peace officer.

He was facing her now:

"Ma'am, what is happening?"

"I don't know."

"What are you doing here?'

She could see his face now; even the light green eyes that bored into her…but somehow not unsympathetically—from thinning, boyish, red hair.

"I…I fell asleep."

She felt like a child, and was quickly becoming as deeply humiliated as she was monstrously relieved.

No, she told herself. *She had done nothing wrong.*

And she was all right now. Whatever had been following her—and some deeply disturbed creature, whatever its nature, had been following her—she was all right now.

Get control of yourself, Nina.

"I fell asleep on the tenth floor. When I woke up…somebody was up there with me."

"What?"

"Someone chased me."

"Who?"

"I don't know."

"Who are you, ma'am?"

"I'm Nina Bannister. I'm a member of Congress."

"My God. Everyone's heard of you, Congresswoman. You're the one who told my wife not to have sex with me on the Fourth of July."

"I'm sorry about that; I really am."

"Who chased you?"

"I don't know. I didn't get a good look at him."

"Did you see a fire?"

"I...no, I...wait!"

"Yes?"

"He was striking matches."

"Striking matches? In the library?"

"Yes, I heard him."

"You didn't see him?"

"No, there were several stacks between him and me. But I heard him; and I smelled the smoke."

After that, the library began to fill up like a supermarket on Saturday morning. The red emergency lights on the walls and ceilings had gone dark now, but were replaced by equally garish and equally red lights outside, as police cars, ambulances, and fire trucks, sirens wailing, stopped beyond the huge plate glass windows that looked out over the campus pond.

Two police officers arrived; civilians, seemingly library personnel, entered through side doors; a security patrolman, dressed differently from the policemen, began walking back and forth, purposefully and uselessly, between the circulation desk and the card file computers.

Nina found herself seated on a wooden chair in the middle of a circle of uniforms, people ostensibly within them, guns hanging beside them, instruments of all kinds—mostly black and shiny though—hanging from them as rattling, blinking, appendages.

The original red-haired officer began questioning her again; but a newly-arrived ex-defensive tackle-turned peace officer—he had to have been a defensive tackle—who could have made two of any of the others in the hall, leaned solicitously toward her, sweat droplets forming on his mocha forehead, which turned from time to time to allow him to glance at the exit from the stairwell.

A policewoman sat close enough to her to put both palms flat upon her knees, acting as a twenty-eight-or-so-year-old mother to fifty-or-so-year-old Nina.

Quietly, patiently, while the library's main floor continued to fill, and the entire area beyond the windows continued to be the Fourth of July, the first officer questioned her again:

"All right, ma'am, I want to be sure I have this right. Your name is…?"

"Nina Bannister."

"You're a member of Congress?"

"Yes. Newly elected."

"And what were you doing in the library?"

"I needed to read. I needed to read a lot. They were nice enough to let me use a carrel up on the tenth floor. My coffee was—I don't know. Something may have been in my coffee. Anyway I went to sleep."

"When?"

"I don't know. I was tired. It must have been a little after nine o'clock."

"No one woke you to tell you the library was closing?"

"No. My carrel, the carrel they let me use, is in a corner; I guess they didn't see me."

"They should," said the young woman, her hands contracting slightly as though to show her displeasure with *they*, whoever *they* were, "have waked you up."

There was nothing to say to that. Silence for a second or so as two women, clearly librarians, came and stood just beyond the ring that was continuing to grow around Nina.

"And when you woke up," Sandy-hair continued, "you saw someone."

"I heard someone."

"Where?"

"About five stacks away from me. I was walking to the elevators."

"The elevators wouldn't have been working at this time of night."

"I know that," she said, trying not to sound impatient, as she realized, somewhat thankfully, that impatience had begun to replace fear as her dominant emotion, "but I knew that stairwells would be unlocked, and that the doors to the stairs were right beside the elevators."

"Congresswoman Bannister," asked the defensive tackle, "do you think that the man you saw…"

"I'm not sure it was a man."

"All right, do you think whoever you saw, is still in the library?"

"I don't know."

"Where did you last see him…or her?"

"In the stairwell."

"At what level?"

"Around level five. I was down here, at the main floor. The person was looking down at me from several landings above."

"Did this person have a weapon?"

"A knife, I think."

"You saw a knife?"

"I heard it."

"You heard it?'

"Yes, it was just…opening and shutting."

"All right," he said, getting to his feet and turning toward the stairwell. "I'm going to check this out."

The red-haired officer looked up at him.

"Take somebody with you."

"Yeah."

The black man turned and walked toward the stairwell entrance.

Some steps away, he was joined by another officer, as thin and weasely as he himself was granite and monumental.

They stood for a time, spoke quietly, and drew their revolvers.

Then they disappeared into the hallway.

After that, a new group of officers appeared in the main entrance of the library.

They wore business suits and looked like executives.

They appeared not to notice the other officers, but spoke only to Nina:

"Congresswoman Bannister?"

"Yes."

"We're from the Secret Service."

And with that, she knew that a new chapter of her life in Washington was beginning.

CHAPTER ELEVEN: THE SECRET SERVICE MAKES ME NERVOUS

The United States Secret Service is headquartered in an ugly nine-story building (The Chesapeake & Potomac Telephone Office Building formerly occupied the structure, until the company went out of business, either because of poor business habits or insanity brought about by the appearance of the building) located at 930 H. Street, N.W.

Nina Bannister and her roommate, the possible next president of the United States, were ushered into the building at 9:30 a.m. on the morning after someone with a cackling voice had pronounced women to be evil and the scourge of God.

She had not slept well, possibly because she had gotten over the drug that had been given to her, or also possibly because she had been chased down library stairs by a lunatic with a knife and it had upset her.

Laurencia Dalrymple had not been in the mood to sleep either, so the two women had sat in the kitchen— where at least they could have access to knives if the need arose—drank coffee (sleep being pretty much impossible anyway) and talked of many things.

Only some of them political.

Nina could, she found herself musing, have been back in Elementals.

Except Laurencia was not Margot nor Alanna, and it was late night and not early morning and it was Washington. DC, and not Bay St Lucy and she was a

Congresswoman and not a retired English teacher, and she had just almost been murdered.

Otherwise, it was all pretty much the same.

And so, here they were, being escorted into one of the scariest buildings she could think of.

It didn't look scary.

It looked like no more than a big train station, or a big bank, with marble floors and old, circa nineteen hundred columns supporting filigreed ceilings.

But it was scary just because it housed the Secret Service.

The Secret Service.

She could only think of President Kennedy's assassination.

She had been a high school student then. A junior. Sitting in the chemistry lab, the chrome-curved faucets over sinks spaced throughout the room, and the Bunsen burners.

James R. Irvin—principal then, as he had been for his entire life—had walked in unexpectedly and taken his place at the front of the room.

His charcoal gray suit a bit frumpy on his tending to overweight frame, and crisscrossed with white chalk marks, for he had been at the black board most of the morning.

He had stood there and said, in his low, rumbling voice:

"I regret to inform all of you that President John Fitzgerald Kennedy has been shot."

Gasps, of course.

"This has just happened in Dallas, Texas. There is no word yet concerning his condition."

Of course, word came soon enough.

This she thought about as she and Laurencia were taken into the elevator and escorted to the seventh floor.

Why, she found herself wondering, *the seventh floor?*

Why not the first, or the ninth?

Strange, the workings of Washington.

The corridor stretched before them, looming, turning, then becoming new corridors, and all the while there was the clacking of shined shoes on shined tiles, and the scarcely perceptible breathing of the two agents flanking them.

"Here we are. Just go on in, and have a seat at the table. Agent Stockmeyer will be with you in just a second."

They did go in, and they did sit, and they did look around.

They were in a circular conference room, and were being looked down upon by all the previous heads of the Secret Service (or at least paintings of them), from the current head all the way back to Theodore Roosevelt.

Who had founded the agency.

"I feel," said Nina, a bit shakily, "like we're going to be sent to prison."

Laurencia merely smiled:

"In a way we are."

"It's my fault."

"Why? Why is it your fault?"

"I don't know. I just always think that whatever it is, it's my fault."

"Nonsense."

"Why did I have to go and visit the library?"

"You're an English teacher. The library is your home. The real question is, why did someone have to put drugs in your coffee and start lecturing you about Eve's sins? At one a.m., I should add."

"Maybe it never happened. Maybe I just dreamed it."

"They found the burned pages, dear."

"Too bad they didn't find him."

"I know."

"Because if he had…"

She was interrupted by the entrance of a tall angular man with a nose like a broken walking stick, and green eyes like Furl. He had on, Nina found herself remarking, the same charcoal suit Mr. Irvin had been wearing on the day of the Kennedy assassination, except that it was a different size, and it had no eraser dust on it, and he was carrying a gun inside it.

A pistol in a shoulder holster, both of which became clearly visible when he reached down to shake their hands.

"Sorry to keep you waiting, Congresswomen."

"That's all right."

"That's all right."

No point in taking issue with a man with a gun.

"I'm Federal Agent Stockmeyer."

Federal Agent Stockmeyer sat down.

"I appreciate your coming in. I know you both have very busy schedules."

"That's all right."

"That's all right."

Great minds, Nina mused, *think alike*.

"We could have had this meeting over at the Capitol building, but it would have been noticed. That's not something we're interested in right now. It's probably good to be as confidential as possible. I'm happy to tell you that we've been able to keep a tight lid on this incident. Except for a few officers from college security, no one knows what happened last night. I must ask both of you to keep it that way."

"We understand," said Laurencia.

"Well, I'll get right to the point. Congresswoman Bannister, we've been unable to locate the man who accosted you last night in the Georgetown Library. We assume that he left the stairwell around the fourth floor, crossed the stacks, and found a back stairwell. By the time the first university security people went up there, he must have been out of the building. Unfortunately, he left nothing behind that might help us get a lead on him."

Nothing to be said to that.

Stockmeyer continued:

"Your Chief of Staff, Congresswoman Bannister, has shown us the letters that have been coming to you. We find them more disturbing than the average crank letter. There are no fingerprints on the envelopes and nothing too distinctive about the word processor that was used to type them. So all we're doing is speculating. But the tone, the style, the method of threat used—all of these fit the profile of an educated man."

"A man?"

"Yes. And probably an older man."

"The one in the library last night?"

A shrug.

"No way to know. We can't rule it out, though. Now, I don't want to be too technical. But it's important that I make this clear. Today, the Secret Service is authorized by law (United States Code 3056) to protect the President, members of his or her family…well, there's a long list. We are also authorized to protect, "major presidential and vice presidential candidates and their spouses within 120 days of a general presidential election. The question is, 'who are major presidential candidates?' Well, the law says any individual identified as such by the Secretary of Homeland Security after consultation with an advisory committee consisting of the Speaker of the House of Representatives, the minority leader of the House of Representatives, the majority and minority leaders of the Senate, and one additional member selected by the other members of the committee."

Stockmeyer paused to let all of the material sink in.

Then he continued, saying:

"I met with those folks this morning."

Laurencia leaned forward and said, in astonishment: "Already?"

A nod.

"This is serious stuff, Madame Congresswoman. We take this incident in the library, as well as the letters in question, to constitute a major threat."

"But according to the law, you can't protect Nina. Or me, for that matter. I feel that I am a serious contender for the presidency."

"And everyone else does, too, Congresswoman."

"Thank you. But it's more than 120 days before the general election."

"Only about a month more. And we're going to bend that rule a little bit."

"Are you allowed to do that?"

"When all the major heads of Congress tell me I'm allowed, then I'm allowed."

He shook his head:

"What national leader worth his or her salt is going to sue us, or cause a stink? 'Let the little woman from Mississippi *be* menaced! We've got to stick by the 120 day rule!' No, I don't think so."

"Well, you may have a point there. Technically though, I haven't received any letters, just Nina."

Stockmeyer leaned forward again.

There was that revolver.

"You've just declared as a candidate for President of The United States. A woman candidate. A founder of this *Lissie* organization. Given what the man has been saying in these letters, we have to assume that he may constitute a threat to you, too."

"I suppose so."

"And, if I may speak in all candor…"

"Please do."

"The situation in the country is now quite—well, *agitated* might be the best word. The July 4th deadline, the gender revolution in terms of political representation—all of these things are very exciting, and you're both to be applauded for them."

"Thank you."

"Thank you."

Great minds again.

"But you have to understand that movements produce counter-movements. *Lissians* are seen by some people, women as well as men, as—well—urging something that is unnatural."

"I have seen the signs on the morning news," said Laurencia, quietly.

"What signs?" asked Nina, who, having finally fallen asleep at four a.m., had missed the broadcasts.

"They have transformed the image of Lysistrata into something resembling a harpy, dear, and they have named her *Lesbo Lissie*."

"Well, that's enterprising of them. Whoever *they* are."

Stockmeyer:

"Some of the meetings, some of the rallies, are becoming violent. It's an interesting phenomenon, though I still find it a scary one. The old issues—abortion rights, gay marriage, gun control—are fading away. People aren't arguing about those things as much. It's gotten down to more of a gut level thing: what does it mean to be feminine or masculine?"

"That," Nina found herself saying, "is gut level all right."

"So the bottom line is, we're going to be assigning some people to both of you."

"How many people?"

"Don't worry about it. We're still making those decisions. The main thing is, your protection will be discreet. Often you won't know anybody's watching you. But you'll each be our responsibility now. And there won't be any more instances like the library."

And with that—at least that and a few cursory words of caution mixed with encouragement, it all coming out to sound like, "Don't worry about a homicidal maniac trying to kill you because we'll be there watching him do it!"—the meeting ended.

A limousine dropped Laurencia outside the Senate building, then continued on to take Nina to her office in the Rayburn building.

She entered, made her way down the crowded hallways, down the stairs of the old building, and finally stopped before the door of her own office.

Which she opened, to reveal eight hard-working people and a chief of staff.

None of them knew about the library.

She greeted everyone, hung up her jacket, and walked back to her own private office.

A stack of letters lay unopened on it.

On top of the stack, though, was a single piece of paper.

Ivory-colored.

She picked it up and read:

I ENJOYED OUR TIME IN THE LIBRARY

CONGRATULATIONS ON YOUR NEW SECURITY BLANKET

CERTAINLY YOU MUST FEEL SAFE NOW.

OH AND BY THE WAY—

TELL LAURENCIA DALRYMPLE TO DROP OUT OF THE RACE

IF SHE DOES NOT DROP OUT BY JULY 14, SHE WILL NOT EXPERIENCE JULY 15.

She stood for a time, stock still, the letter shaking in her hand.

Then she sat down, put her face in her hands, and attempted not to cry.

CHAPTER TWELVE: BUSTER THE BEAGLE AND THE TWO DOLLS

Nina was loathe to let the bizarre experience in the university library sour her on Georgetown completely, so the following day she splurged and took a cab to 31st and R Street, which she had learned was the most convenient entrance to the magical world that was Dumbarton Oaks. She had been told of the place early on in her Washington D.C. life, and this would be her fourth visit. For some reason, she could not stay away. Dumbarton Oaks was, of course, really three gardens in one: a wild and tangled English garden, a mathematical French garden, and a magnificent rose garden. There was a stunning collection of terraces, tree-shaded brick walks, fountains, arbors, and pools.

There were also running trails, and, if she ever needed a good slow jog to rid her mind of disturbing memories, it was now.

And so, this particular morning she had pulled on her black *Lissie* t-shirt (letter writer be damned), her red shorts, her battered jogging shoes, and her floppy hat—and gone for it!

She was now half a mile from the park's main entrance and chugging along at almost the speed she would have attained on her Vespa, if her Vespa were here.

She missed, she realized as she eyed longingly a bench that was still over a hundred yards away, her Vespa.

But then again, she missed her cat, although it was not certain that Furl missed her, since he was being taken care of by Jackson Bennett and his daughters.

She missed the ocean, and her shack.

She missed Margot's visits, and the puttering around in Elementals that she had become accustomed to.

Instead, she had this bizarre existence that was proving to be nothing like she had expected.

Was it a dream?

The fact that she could have been elected as a temporary replacement in the United States House of Representatives was strange enough; but the events of the last week, the viralization of her sex tirade, the formation of the Lissie Movement, the nationwide protests and counter-protests, the fervor that this gender revolution was making...

...no, she half expected to wake up, her head still lying on the table on her oceanside deck, the waves growling beneath her, and Furl rubbing her ankles, looking up angrily as if to yowl:

Rrrgggh.

Or...

Stop dozing and feed me!

She had halved the distance to the bench when another animal entered her life, this time from behind, at the same instant she heard another voice cry out:

"No! No, Buster! Buster come back here!"

Buster did not come back to the source of the voice, though, because he, trailing his leash, had overtaken Nina and was bounding joyfully at her right leg, licking her knee, and doing his best to tell her that he absolutely loved her.

She returned some of this love, at least—although she could not pant quite as heartily as Buster could—because the intrusion into her life of this mammoth beagle was making it impossible for her to run, and for that, at least, she was immensely thankful.

"Buster, leave the lady alone."

Buster had no intention at all of doing that.

Instead, he continued to stand on his back two paws, his tongue about at her navel level now, his white-tipped tail churning back and forth in the rose-scented early summer air, and his eyes bright with the realization that:

"I HAVE MADE A NEW FRIEND!"

"Stop that!"

The source of the voice—and, quite probably the owner of the dog—approached as fast as she could, which was not too fast, given that she was pushing a double-seated baby stroller before her, while grasping futilely at the other end of Buster's black leather collar.

"I'm sorry! I'm so sorry!"

"Oh don't worry about it!" Nina said, laughing back at the laughing Buster, but not drooling as much—she hoped—as he was.

"He's so strong—I couldn't hold onto his leash!"

The woman who had failed so miserably at restraining her animal was probably in her mid-twenties, also appareled for jogging—almost everyone in Dumbarton Oaks at ten o'clock this morning was there for jogging, Nina noted—Hispanic, and quite beautiful.

She had long lustrous glowing black hair that came almost to the middle of her back, and her raven eyes sparkled as she smiled.

Nina could not help thinking of Sonia Ramirez, and wondering as she did so if this young woman was a basketball player too.

Some kind of a ball player she must have been—or some kind of a gymnast or swimmer or runner or whatever—for her body had that look about it that said

"I'm out here running, although I don't need it at all and would look this fit and strong even if I never ran another day in my life."

That look.

"I'm Sylvia Morales. And—wait—are you Nina Bannister?"

"Yes, I am."

"Oh, my God! You're my idol!"

"Oh, don't be silly!"

"No, you are, you really are! I'm a Lissie! I didn't wear my black shirt this morning! But I'm still a Lissie and many of my friends are, too. We talk about you all the time, and the great speech you gave!"

"I'm flattered!"

"No. I'm the one who should be flattered! My dog Buster almost ran over one of the most famous women in Washington!"

As for Buster, he was still going at it, and it was all Nina could do to keep her palms pressed hard enough on his glossy aircraft carrier back to satisfy him.

"Would you give me your autograph?"

This shocked Nina somewhat, because she had never been asked for her autograph before, and so it took an instant or so for her to recover her composure and answer:

"Yes, I'd be happy to."

"Ok, then, here—let me get this little wallet I carry out of my jogging pants—and, here, I've got a pen, too—"

Nina watched her search for these articles, and noticed, as she did so, the two children who were riding quietly in the double stroller.

They were almost completely covered beneath a neatly folded red blanket.

Their faces were angelic, and the long wispy eye lashes extended from their cornflower blue eyes fluttered ever so slightly in the breeze that was easing its way through the park.

These things Nina noted even before the realization hit her that they were not children at all.

They were dolls.

Just toy store dolls with radiant blonde hair and WHITEWHITEWHITEWHITE skin.

Making Nina think:

Oh great. I've run into another looney.

The university library. Dumbarton Oaks.

Maybe it's just Georgetown.

Better go up to Foggy Bottom. Or just stay home.

"Here. If you could sign the back of this business card." Nina took the card and looked at it, half expecting to read the words:

PROFESSIONAL IDIOT

What she did read, however, were the words:

SYLVIA MORALES

AGENT

UNITED STATES SECRET SERVICE

"Just turn it over, and sign the back, if you will."

"Sure."

Nina did so, saying:

"That explains a few things. Like your *children* there."

"Aren't they just dolls?"

"That's extremely well put. Here."

She handed back the card.

"We're going to be watching out for you," said Sylvia, quietly, "from now until the election. You may not always see us. In fact, if you're too aware of us, then we probably aren't doing our jobs very well."

"You really think I'm in danger?"

A shrug.

"There are a lot of crazy people out there. Apparently one of them has been writing letters. We tried to find fingerprints on the letters that showed up in your office yesterday. No luck. The scary thing, of course, is how he could have gotten in there."

"Yes."

"And the thing in the library. By the way, that's still being kept completely confidential. No one knows about it. I'm assuming you haven't talked about it."

"No. Not a word."

"Good. Well, Nina, try not to worry. You're in good hands now, I promise."

"So—you, like—I mean, could you kill somebody with your bare hands?"

"No, but this dog could."

"I feel safer already."

"Damn straight. Now, I hear that you're going over to George Washington University tonight."

And that was true.

No faulting the Secret Service on their Intelligence Gathering Branch.

"I am. Laurencia set it up a few days ago. There is a professor there named Morgana Davis. She teaches a class in Women in Literature. Apparently, the students want to know more about me, and about what I'm doing here in Washington, and how the *Lissie* movement came about."

"I want to know more about all those things too. So I'm going to be in the class when you talk. I called Professor Davis this morning and asked if I could sit in."

"Did you tell her you were in the Secret Service?"

"If I did that, it wouldn't be a secret anymore."

"I guess that makes sense."

"But you need to realize, anytime you speak before a crowd now…well, I or one of my colleagues will have your back."

"That's good to know, Sylvia. I appreciate it. And so does Laurencia, I'm sure."

"Just doing our jobs."

"Are the two kids coming tonight?"

"They're a little young for advanced feminist studies."

"There's that to think about. That and the fact that they're not real human beings."

Sylvia shook her head and straightened the blanket covering Doll #1:

"That never seemed to be a problem for a lot of the professors I used to know in college."

"You have a point."

"Nice to have met you, Nina Bannister. I hope to see you more in the future. But I also hope you won't be seeing me."

"Vaya," said Nina, Olivia Ramirez' words flashing into her mind as she spoke, "con Dios."

The Federal Agent beamed back at her:

"Y usted, Nina. Y usted."

So saying, she turned and, two plastic children in front of her and one overweight beagle behind her, walked away.

George Washington University, having no campus of its own, is a mélange of modern office buildings and nineteenth-century houses between 19th and 24th streets south of Pennsylvania Avenue.

Still, as the sun set around seven o'clock and streetlights began to come on, there was a collegial feel as Nina walked with Laurencia toward Briarwood Hall, where she was to speak. Students were everywhere, and there were still open spaces of ground where Frisbees could be thrown and dogs could launch themselves high in the air to catch them.

"How do you know Professor Davis, Laurencia?"

The woman beside her smiled:

"I took a class at the University when I was still a young congresswoman. It was essentially the same class she teaches now. We're a bit early; she'll be finishing up her lecture. She told me she wanted to divide the class in two halves; she'll be lecturing for the first half, and then you'll have half an hour or so to make remarks and answer the students' questions. So I hurried a bit more than might have been absolutely necessary. I wanted you to hear Morgana. Ah—here we are, just over there."

They turned a corner and Nina could see Briarwood Hall.

Her heartbeat quickened a bit.

It was not one of the sterile black and white office buildings they had been passing through. Rather, it had the red brick solidity and ornamentation that one associated with elegance and taste.

One made money in office buildings. After having done so, one lived comfortably in one of these buildings.

"Through here."

"All right."

Laurencia led the way into the building, and then up a flight of stairs.

"Now, down this corridor. It's Lecture Hall 222. The same place she taught in when I took the course."

It was late in the day, and the corridor before them was almost deserted. But Nina could hear the sound of a woman's voice from two doors in front of them.

They paused briefly in front of Room 222, then Laurencia opened the door.

A marvelous lecture hall smiled back at them, with concentric rows of seats leading down to the podium around which Morgana Davis was pacing, and a massive wall of windows to the left letting in the last rays of the setting sun.

The woman at the podium was tall, straight, and silver haired. She walked with the aid of cane, which was also tall and straight and silver, and her smile flashed like the sunlight as she raised her head and shouted:

"Hail and well met, my colleagues!"

Laurencia shouted back:

"Room here for two old ladies?"

Laughter from the students who filled the hall.

Laughter too from Morgana Davis, who then continued:

"Please, Congresswoman Bannister, come on down! Nina Bannister, I'm quite sure, is known to all of you, and especially those of you wearing black shirts. Please, Congresswoman Bannister, the floor is yours!"

A huge cheer.

Nina could feel herself blushing.

She made her way down to the podium, smiled at Sylvia, and waited for the applause to die down.

"I want to thank you for asking me to speak," she said. I hardly knew, when I got the invitation, what I was going to say. But I was reading a book the other night…"

She glanced at Sylvia.

The book was one she had been poring over in the Georgetown Library when she had been drugged.

She had found it again downtown, and had bought it.

"You're all brilliant students, and you have a wonderful professor. You may already know this book by heart. I didn't know it, though. And when I began reading it, it made me feel as though I wasn't crazy. That all of those things I said in that recording—well, that they might really be true. So, if I have your permission, I want to read a few excerpts."

"Of course," shouted Morgana Davis, "you have our permission!"

"All right. Here then are some lines from Dee Dee Myers' book, *Why Women Should Rule the World*.

Cheering.

"Ms. Myers, of course, was the press secretary for President Bill Clinton. She writes:"

"If we were in charge, things might actually change. Instead of posturing, we'd have cooperation. Instead of gridlock, we'd have progress. Instead of a shouting match, we'd have a conversation. A very long conversation."

And she writes:

"I found myself more and more frustrated by the bitterness that now gripped the capital. Increasingly, it seemed, both sides were more interested in winning the argument than solving the problem. And the result was gridlock, polarization, and cynicism."

"Was anyone talking and listening to each other?"

"And I realized that *yes,* some people were. And one of the places that that seemed to be happening on a regular basis was among the *women in The United States Senate.*"

Pause.

Nina put the book down and pointed to the back row.

"I can tell you that, right now, one of the reasons for that spirit of co-operation is here with us tonight. It's Laurencia Dalrymple."

Everyone in the room stood and cheered.

And the cheering kept up until Laurencia forced it to stop by gesturing *enough*.

Hands were waving in the air now, though, and it seemed the right time to take a question.

"Yes?"

"Congresswoman Bannister, how do you answer the accusation that you 'hate men?'"

Laughter.

Nina laughed too.

She was expecting that.

"I don't have any worries on that score. For twenty-seven years I was married to…"

A movement in front of her and to the right caught her eye.

Sylvia Morales was standing now and screaming:

"Get down! Get down!"

She stared as though paralyzed.

"Dammit, Nina, get down!"

"I don't…"

But before she could finish, the young agent had rounded the row of stadium chairs, bounded three strides toward the podium, and hurled her body into Nina's.

She could feel her ribs seem to cave in, and felt her forehead smash against the tile floor just as the entire wall of windows exploded and she was covered by raining pellets of plate glass.

CHAPTER THIRTEEN: THE LIFE OF THE MIND

Pandemonium.

Everyone in the hall seemed to be screaming and running for the two exits. Around her, Nina was aware of glittering pellets of glass, like hailstones covering the floor.

Sylvia Morales lay flat on top of her, so she could neither move nor turn her head. She heard the click of what she assumed was a radio of some sort, and Sylvia's voice, as calm as the voice of someone ordering groceries by telephone.

"We have a shooter in the office building adjacent to Briarwood Hall. One shot has been fired. No injuries. Repeat: shooter is inside the office building adjacent to Briarwood Hall."

Suddenly, the weight that had been pressing Nina's back and face to the floor disappeared, and she corkscrewed around in time to see Sylvia jumping up and shouting:

"Stay in the room! Do not exit! Stay in the room!"

This did not have the effect of keeping everyone in the room, because the doors had been opened and a few people had escaped, but it did slow the mass exodus, and it did seem to quieten the screaming slightly.

Nina got to her knees.

The massive window was gone, or at least transformed into a carpet of glass pellets and shards that covered the area around the podium.

Sylvia continued to shout at the students:

"Stay where you are! Do not leave the room! Take cover, if you can, behind the desks!"

She also continued to speak into what Nina now took to be a kind of two-way transmitter that she had pulled from her purse.

"We need backup immediately! Shots have been fired. Shooter is almost certainly still in the office building immediately adjacent to Briarwood Hall on the campus of George Washington University. Target is unharmed. Repeat: target is unharmed."

Then she looked down at Nina:

"Are you all right?"

Nina could not speak.

The strangest sensation.

Whatever muscles connected her brain and her mouth had become useless, paralyzed.

She could only move her head uselessly from side to side, and then up and down.

She felt like a department store mannequin.

"Nina, are you all right?"

Again, no speech.

She supposed she was in shock.

But she did have the presence of mind enough to feel her legs, to move her arms, to rub the palms of her hands over her cheeks and jaws.

Finally, words came out.

"I...I...think I'm all right."

"Just take slow, even breaths. See if you can move your arms and legs."

She did these things, then said:

"I'm all right. I'm sure of it now."

"All right. Then don't stand up. Move—crawl—behind the podium, so that it's between you and the window, and between you and the door."

She lurched along on all fours until the wooden podium was blocking her sight of most of the room.

She still could peek around a corner of the stand though and see Sylvia, who was making her way up the aisle toward the back of the hall, pushing through sobbing students as she did so.

"Stay in the hall! Do not go out into the corridor!"

Then she began to hear students alternately screaming and shouting out questions:

"My God! My God! What's happening?"

"We've got to get out of here!"

"Let us go; let us go!"

But Sylvia had by this time posted herself against the wall and between the two doors that let out of the room. She reached behind her and pulled out a black, shiny .45 automatic—Nina knew that's what it was because it was the same gun Penelope Royale carried in her boat.

"Now listen to me. Everybody, listen to me!"

"Who are you?"

"What is happening here?"

"My God! My God, let us out!"

Sylvia merely shook her head and said, as calmly as possible under the circumstances:

"You have to listen to me. My name is Sylvia Morales. I'm an agent of the United States Secret Service. I don't want you to panic, but you do have to know what is happening. An attempt has been made on the life of Congresswoman Bannister. The shooter apparently was located in the fourth floor of the office building next to Briarwood. Only one shot was fired. Congresswoman Bannister is all right. No one has been hurt."

"Why can't we get out of here?"

"What if he comes in here? Why can't we leave?"

Another shake of the head:

"We don't know where he is at this moment. If you start running down the halls, you may meet him."

"He's coming here?"

"We don't know that. We don't know where he is or what his intentions are. We have to assume though that he is still armed and dangerous."

"But what if he comes in here?"

A short pause and then Sylvia Morales said:

"If he comes in here, I'll kill him."

There was very little to be said to that.

Nina could see Sylvia, standing ramrod straight, positioned precisely between the two doors, looking first at one, then at the other.

She had never felt so safe in her life.

The next fifteen to twenty minutes reminded Nina of the time following her escape at the library, except much more so. Sirens were going off all over the campus. Students moved in pairs and other small groups, arms around each other, mouths opened in shocked silence. And everyone seemed to be realizing the falsity of that comforting, but never really true, statement:

"It can't happen here."

Columbine.

Sandy Hook.

Different of course, because here no one had been injured.

But still…

"Here, dear. You've got to get some coffee in you."

"Thank you, Laurencia."

The two of them had been moved by other officers—uniformed guards had been pouring into the building for some time now—and were seated in the front row of what Nina assumed was a regular classroom.

Blackboard.

No windows.

Every two minutes, another officer wearing a different uniform would park himself in front of her, look her straight in the eye, and ask:

"Are you certain you're ok?"

To which she would merely nod and say:

"I'm fine."

She was getting a little sick of it.

Finally, the ebb and flow of Protective Personnel stabilized a bit, and Nina realized that she and Laurencia were in something like command central.

Sylvia had re-materialized, and was sitting two seats away from them, smiling reassuringly.

There were three other agents in the room—all men, all dressed in business suits.

These were, Nina assumed, all secret service agents.

And at the front of the room, seated behind the teacher's desk, was Stockmeyer.

He cleared his throat.

The soft mumblings of conversation stopped.

"All right. Things seem to have calmed down somewhat, and I'd like to be sure everyone knows where we are. First, Congresswoman Bannister: are you all right?"

It would have been improper to smile, so Nina did not do so.

"Yes. I'm fine. Thanks to Sylvia."

"Senator Dalrymple?"

A nod.

"I'm fine, Agent Stockmeyer. No one was shooting at me."

"No, but the letters have been referencing you. We have to assume that you are a potential target as well."

To this, Laurencia actually did smile.

Senators, Nina mused, *can pull off things Representatives can't.*

At least, temporary representatives.

"Target," said Laurencia, quietly. "There's something so reassuring about that term."

"I'm sorry to put it that way. It's just…"

"It's just true."

"Yes. Unfortunately. And, I must tell you because you need to know. We were not able to apprehend the suspect. The closest law enforcement officials to the building in question were campus security, and they took about two minutes to get there. That was sufficient time for the shooter to flee the building."

Silence for a time.

Then Stockmeyer:

"Now, Agent Morales. Tell us what happened."

Sylvia leaned forward on her desk.

"Nina had been speaking for maybe five minutes. I saw something kind of sparkle out of the corner of my eye. I looked over at the office building and saw the rifle barrel glinting in the sun. I shouted. Then I was able to get around the row of seats and make a dive for her. I covered her just as the window shattered. The next thing I realized, we were on the ground. I don't know where the bullet went."

"Did you see that the building was over there, and that there were numerous windows in it before the Congresswoman began to speak?"

"Yes."

"And yet you let her proceed?"

"I'm sorry, sir. A rookie's mistake. A trainee's mistake. I should have either had the podium moved to a more secure place in the hall, or insisted that the speech take place in a different room, with no windows."

"We'll talk about that later."

"Yes, sir."

"All right. Then tell me…"

Nina interrupted.

She surprised herself by doing so.

But she had to know.

"Where did," she asked, quietly, "the bullet actually go?"

Stockmeyer shook his head:

"That's not really important in our…"

"Where did it go?"

A pause.

Then:

"It went into the wall four feet behind the podium."

"So it passed through where my head would have been."

"Yes."

Nina got up, took two steps, bent down and embraced Sylvia.

"Thank you. Thank you."

Both of them had tears in their eyes.

Nina's encounter in the Georgetown University Library had garnered little in the way of public attention. Nothing had actually happened, other than a few books being defaced.

The *shooting* at George Washington University, as the event almost immediately became labeled, was a different matter.

It would have been big news had no political figure been involved.

As it was..

Protests and marches sprang up again, with Lissies shouting and singing and screaming support for Nina Bannister, who had come within a split second of being a martyr for the cause of women's rights.

The thing was all over the Social Network.

Students who had been in the hall were being interviewed, and were telling, of course, wildly differing accounts of what had actually happened.

By seven o'clock in the evening, Nina and her roommate were sitting in the kitchen of their apartment—somehow this had become their favorite place of all—having a glass of white wine.

They had, they decided, earned it.

The apartment was surrounded by security personnel.

Her entire life, Nina now assumed, would be surrounded by security personnel.

They were surprised then to hear a knock at the door.

Nina looked at Laurencia:

"Reporters?"

Laurencia shook her head.

"Reporters are banned. The security people won't let them come up."

"Then who?"

"I haven't the slightest idea."

"Should we open the door?"

Laurencia got to her feet:

"I may," she said, "be a target, and people may be shooting at my new friend with deer rifles. But I will not be too damned frightened to open the door of my own apartment."

So that is what she did.

Revealing Sylvia Morales, who stood just outside the door.

"Sorry to bother both of you."

"Come in, Sylvia!"

In a minute's time, all three of them were seated at the table, and another glass of cold wine had been poured.

"I'm not supposed to be up here. But I knew someone on the detail down below, and I bribed him."

"Why," asked Nina, "are you not supposed to be up here? You're our security detail."

"Not any more."

"What?"

"No. I was removed."

'Removed from what?"

"From being on your protection team."

"That's ridiculous! You saved my life! That was one of the bravest things I've ever seen! I would be dead by now if it weren't for you!"

But Sylvia merely shook her head and said:

"None of it should have happened. A huge open window like that, with a massive building next door, lots of offices—it's Protection 101. You were a sitting duck."

"So they're firing you?"

She shrugged:

"We'll see. The main thing is—well, it's just sad. Because I like both of you. And I'd like to have continued working with you."

"Wait a minute, wait a minute," said Nina. "Surely we have some say in who our agent is! And we want you! We'll call Stockmeyer and insist!"

A shake of the head:

"Not the Secret Service. He pretty much does as he wants."

But Laurencia was taking out her cell phone and dialing it.

"Perhaps we can change his attitude."

"I appreciate it, Senator, but if you're calling Stockmeyer on my behalf…"

"I'm not calling Stockmeyer."

A pause while she listened, the phone to her ear.

Finally, she said:

"This is Laurencia Dalrymple. Is he available?"

A pause. Then:

"Excellent. I'm so fortunate. Please tell him I'm calling in a favor. Give him this number. Tell him I'll be waiting. Thank you."

She flipped the phone shut.

"Now. Let's wait a bit. I believe I'll have some more wine. Nina?"

"No, I've had plenty."

"Sylvia?"

"On duty."

"Just as you wish."

She had finished pouring her second glass when the phone rang.

She flipped it open and said into it:

"Thank you so much for calling me back. I have a favor to ask, especially if you have any pull with the Secret Service."

She was silent for a time, then smiled and said:

"Well I would think so too. We have a wonderful agent assigned to us. Sylvia Morales is her name. She saved Nina's life today, and, for that, as a reward, she has been replaced."

Silence.

Then:

"I know. It's insane. But the bottom line is we love her, and we feel safe being in her protection. We don't want another agent. So if you could…ah. Ah, yes, that would be wonderful. Thank you."

And, so saying, she hung up.

"Who was that?" asked Nina.

"A friend with some power. I've been in Washington a good bit longer than he, and so I've been able to do several favors for him. Now perhaps he can do one for us. At any rate, we shall see. Let's simply enjoy our wine for a bit. And while we do so…"

The phone rang.

Laurencia handed it to Sylvia:

"I feel certain it's for you, honey."

Sylvia took it and said into it:

"Agent Morales here."

Silence.

Then:

"Yes, sir. Yes, sir, I understand. And I appreciate it greatly. Yes. Yes, of course."

She hung up, then turned, and, beaming, said to Nina:

"I've been reinstated! That was Stockmeyer! He's decided to give me a second chance!"

"Wonderful!" shouted Nina.

And the phone rang yet again.

Laurencia:

"Yes. Yes, she's back. Thank you so much!"

Pause.

"Oh yes, she is here. I'll let you speak to her."

Laurencia handed the phone to Sylvia, who listened for a moment and finally said:

"Thank you, sir. I was just doing my job."

Pause.

Sylvia:

"Nina, he wants to talk to you."

"Who…"

"Here. Just listen."

Nina took the phone.

She did listen.

Finally, she said:

"No, sir. I'm quite all right. And yes, sir. I'm proud of the *Lissie* movement too."

She listened for a time longer, said a few words, she hardly remembered what they were.

Then she hung up.

Laurencia and Sylvia were both smiling at her.

"That," she said, smiling back at them, "was the President of The United States."

CHAPTER FOURTEEN: ROLL DOWN LIKE WATERS

There was no sleep for either of them, of course, but there was a decision made. Nina made it at around four in the morning, while she was thrashing around in bed, reliving the previous hours.

She told it to Laurencia over a very early breakfast—for her roommate could not sleep either—while they were eating bran flakes covered with milk and blueberries, and drinking coffee.

The sun had not yet risen, nor had gray flakes begun to appear in the sky.

The neighborhood was relatively quiet. A siren in the distance; a dog barking somewhere down the street.

Outside, the security vehicles had made themselves invisible.

But they were there.

And they would always be there.

For—how long, for God's sake?

"I have to quit," Nina was saying.

Laurencia looked at her, but did not seem surprised.

"Quit and do what?"

"Go home."

"Why?"

Nina looked back and did seem surprised, but only because she was.

"What do you mean, 'why?'"

"Just what I asked."

"Laurencia, this idiot shot at me."

"Yes, I know. I was there."

"The bullet could have blown up my head! "

"But it didn't."

"No, but next time..."

'You're sure there's going to be a next time?"

"That's just it, Laurencia. Maybe if I quit, there won't be. This nut obviously thinks I'm doing something against the will of God. If I stop, maybe he will, too."

"Then he will have won."

"And I'll still be alive."

"Yes. You will be."

Nina leaned forward on the table.

"Laurencia, I don't want to be a martyr. I'm not meant to be. I'm not a famous person, or at least I haven't lived my life that way. I came here to Washington because a lot of people asked me to, and because I thought I could make a difference, just a little difference."

"A little difference."

"Yes, and that's all. Now people are beginning to look at me as some kind of Gender Messiah."

"Because to them you are."

"But why can't somebody else be, for a while? Why do I have to spend the next part of my life, for I don't know how many months, terrified to sit by a window, and diving under the bed every time a tire blows out?"

Laurencia thought about that for a time and then said:

"You have a point. If you went back to Bay St. Lucy, maybe the guy would be satisfied. Maybe all the guys would be satisfied, and maybe the Lissie movement would just die out for lack of a leader."

"I don't think..."

"Tell you what, Nina. Let me take you somewhere."

"Where?"

"One of my favorite places in Washington. We have the limo here that the Secret Service has assigned to us. They'll take us now if we want to go."

"So early?"

"This place never closes. I go there often before sunrise, to experience the dawn. Come on. I'll show it to you."

So Nina finished dressing, and, five minutes later, she was driving down West Basin Drive, to the Martin Luther King Memorial.

She had not seen it close up, but it astonished her when they got out of the limo.

It was more impressive in the dark, both it and the granite blocks it had been hewn from, glowing white in searchlights installed at its base.

"It's like Rushmore," she whispered to Laurencia. "That massive white statue, carved out of the limestone mountain behind it, containing it."

Laurencia shook her head:

"Not limestone. No, the sculpture was carved from 159 blocks of granite that were assembled to appear as one singular piece. The whole thing is meant to convey the three themes that were central throughout Dr. King's life. Democracy, justice and hope. The statue is thirty feet high and known as the Stone of Hope." Dr. King is carved gazing out over the horizon—where the sun will come up, actually—and concentrating on the future and the hope of humanity. To the side is a 450-foot inscription wall, made from granite panels. It's inscribed with fourteen excerpts from Dr. King's sermons and public addresses. Come on. Let's just walk around the memorial, and read.

They did, Laurencia leading, Nina a step or so behind.

They were alone at the memorial. To their left loomed the Washington Monument, and directly across the Tidal Basin, the Thomas Jefferson Memorial.

But these things seemed almost unimportant compared to the words carved into white granite in front of her:

"Let justice roll down like waters and righteousness like a mighty stream."

And:

"Out of the mountain of despair, a stone of hope."

And:

"Injustice anywhere is a threat to justice everywhere. We are caught in an inescapable network of mutuality, tied in a single garment of destiny. Whatever affects one directly, affects all indirectly."

And:

"Make a career of humanity. Commit yourself to the noble struggle for equal rights. You will make a better person of yourself, a greater nation of your country, and a finer world to live in."

And finally, Laurencia said:

"I think this is my favorite, here on the North Wall. It's from *Strength to Love*, and he made the speech in 1963. He had five years left to live. Then he was shot. He probably knew he was going to get shot. It had to happen. And so he said:

"The ultimate measure of a man is not where he stands in moments of convenience and comfort, but where he stands at times of challenge and controversy."

After a time, they both sat down on the moist granite stones.

The sun was coming up now, and they could see faint streaks of saffron gold coming up over the Jefferson Memorial, and reflecting in the wading pool.

"Of course," Laurencia said, quietly, "he said 'a man.' He probably wouldn't have meant for the sayings to apply to you and me."

Nina shook her head slowly, and smiled.

"No. Of course not. We're just women."

They were silent for a time longer.

Then Nina said:

"Come on."

"Where are we going?"

"Home, of course. I have to change and get to work."

And they left.

By the time Nina had arrived at the Rayburn Building, the corridors had already begun to fill up with other congressional staff personnel.

She had to fight through them to get to her own office and push open the door.

The room in front of her seemed, at first, deserted.

Then she saw movement at a desk in a cluttered corner.

Dicken Proctor arose and stared at her.

He said nothing.

All of the three rooms of her office were deathly silent.

"Dicken, what is it?"

He continued to stare.

She stepped into the office, then repeated:

"What is it? Where is the rest of the staff?"

He shook his head slowly:

"I sent them home. They started arriving about half an hour ago. And I sent them home."

"Why?"

He circled around to the center of the room.

He took another step toward her.

His mouth was gaping.

"I got here at six. Before everybody else. And I found this letter, on the desk back in your main office."

He handed it to her.

She read:

I'M SORRY I MISSED. I WILL NOT MISS AGAIN.

Nina took a deep breath and said:

"He got in here again."

"Yes. He did."

"How is that possible?"

Dicken looked even more horrified and whispered:

"It's possible because he was able to get a key. He has a master key to all the offices. He told me that once."

"What? Dicken, what in God's name are you talking about?"

"It's not in God's name. It couldn't be!"

"What are you *talking* about?"

"Nina—I saw him! When I got here, the man writing these letters—he was here! In here, back in your office! He was laying the letter gently on the desk. And when I walked in—he looked up at me! I saw him!"

"But Dicken...why didn't you try to stop him?"

"I...I couldn't."

"And so you just let him leave?"

"Yes. It was as though I couldn't move."

"That's crazy! Why didn't you call security?"

"I..I.."

"Have you called security now?"

"No, because he..."

"He's what, dammit?"

Another step forward, then:

"Because he's dead!"

"*Who* is dead?"

"The man who left the letter."

"That's insane!"

"Nina…"
And then a slow shake of the head:
"The man who left the letter…is Jarrod Thornbloom.

CHAPTER FIFTEEN: THE MAN WHO LOVED DICKEN

The office into which Nina Bannister had been moved was everything Mississippi. It was FOOTBALL FOOTBALL FOOTBALL with balls, jerseys, helmets, overview pictures, newspapers headlines, shoes, face guards—and it was COTTON COTTON COTTON, with an actual bale stuffed somehow not quite into a corner, and photos of cotton gins with their yards filled with wagons.

It was FAULKNER FAULKNER FAULKNER with an entire portion of the west wall built as a shrine to the Nobel laureate who had created a mythical Yoknapatawpha county and a world of Snopeses (Flem Snopes, Montgomery Ward Snopes, etc.) to populate it.

It was trinkets and Civil War memorabilia and Robert E. Lee and marlin caught off Bay St. Lucy and deer shot near Meridian and—

—well, it just went on and on and on.

Except that it had been gradually collected over the decades by Jarrod Thornbloom for his seventeen acres of office space.

Then it had been crammed down here into the basement of the Rayburn Building and compacted into Nina's cubic foot and a half of office space.

So there really wasn't much a place to sit. Or walk. Or work.

Or breathe standing straight.

It was hard with eight aides and Dicken Proctor.

It was easier, though, when one was alone.

As Nina now found herself.

After "The Proctorlamation" as it had quickly become known (*Proctor Proclamation*, with a bit of language stretching thrown in) had reached the Secret Service (five minutes) all Hell had broken loose.

Of course, at least in Nina's mind all Hell had broken loose from the time of her viralization, and she was having a hard time remembering which part of loose Hell she was dealing with any one time.

But that really didn't take too much concentration.

She wasn't dealing with an enigmatic, shadowy figure in the Georgetown Library.

She wasn't dealing with an assassination attempt and a floor covered by shattered window glass.

Those would have been hard enough.

She was dealing with—they all were dealing with—a ghost.

A man whose private jet had crashed into the Atlantic Ocean a thousand miles from the shore of the United States of America and three thousand miles from the shore of France...

...and had still turned up here, in this office, seven hours ago.

For it was now 2 p.m.

She had been here all alone all that time.

They had told her to stay here, and that was that.

Several agents had explained it all in the following way:

She could not be sent home, to the apartment she shared with Laurencia, because, after the shooting at George Washington, a sea of media personnel had spread slowly around the place, and all efforts to remove them—these were, after all, public streets—had proved useless.

A quiet, boutique hotel?

Impossible.

She was too closely watched now.

Business as usual?

No, business was not as usual. Her staff had been sent home. They needed to stay home, at least for the day.

And so she had been told to stay here, where she could be very tightly guarded.

Outside, in the corridors, business did go on pretty much as usual.

So a thousand or so security people were engaged to float up and down the hallways of the Rayburn Building, but they managed to look like they were doing what everybody else was doing—fundraising or glad-handing—and so no one much minded them.

Nina simply drank one cup of coffee after another, sat at her big desk, and read.

What did she read?

Faulkner, of course.

She did this for several hours.

A Rose for Emily was actually pretty believable when one compared it to what her chief of staff had just reported.

Emily Grierson had slept with a dead man for ten years or so, but at least he had shown the courtesy of staying dead and rotting.

This Jarrod Thornbloom on the other hand, well, that was a different story.

Finally, at just after two o'clock in the afternoon, the door was opened (by a real person and not a deceased one) just as she had been apprised that it would be.

Sylvia Morales entered.

The two women hugged, sobbed, hugged again, laughed a little, and sat down.

They asked each other whether they were doing all right and, yes, they were, in fact, doing all right and the weather was good and etc. etc.

Finally, Nina asked:

"So what's been going on?"

Sylvia took a deep breath.

This was going to take a while.

"All right. As soon as word got over to Stockmeyer, three agents came and got Proctor. They took him immediately to the Service headquarters. He hasn't seen anybody but Service people since he saw this…"

"…this ghost."

"Well, yeah, whatever it is he saw. The main thing is, the press can't be told about this. That's why you've been kept here…"

"Like a prisoner."

"You're not a prisoner. Stockmeyer wanted me to stress that to you."

"I'm not a prisoner?"

"No, you're just a person who has to stay in one place and isn't allowed to go anywhere else."

"Oh. Thanks for clearing that up for me."

"There are just too many people out there who want to talk to you, Nina. And you're too honest."

"I can lie if I want to."

"Have you ever lied?"

"Well, maybe not, but I've been wrong."

"See, that isn't the same thing."

"Same result."

"The problem is, you wouldn't have been wrong on this. If somebody had asked you, did your Chief of Staff see Jarrod Thornbloom a few hours ago, you would have said *yes*. And then everything would have been chaos."

"As opposed to now, when everything is…"

"Just impossible."

"Ok, tell me more."

"Well, Proctor got sent into the interrogation room with Stockmeyer and two other agents."

'You being one of them?"

"Yes. A word from the President makes a lot of difference. I'm hot stuff now."

"Glad to hear it."

"Question after question: what was he wearing? What did he say to you? Have you been drinking? Do you take drugs? Do you realize that what you claim you *saw* is impossible?"

"And Proctor?"

"Poor guy. Probably never been interrogated like that. By pros, I mean. I thought he was going to break into tears. But he just sat there, and kept on nodding, and keeping control of himself, and repeating the same thing: 'I tell you I saw Jarrod Thornbloom.'"

"So what happened?"

Sylvia shrugged:

"What happened was, the whole crash investigation got re-opened. Calls went flying to Dulles Airport. By ten o'clock, where Proctor had been sitting, Stockmeyer had the guys who had testified after the initial crash. Two controllers who had been in the tower, and the mechanic who had serviced Thornbloom's plane. And it was the same story that they had told earlier, I guess."

"You weren't around for their original testimony?"

"No, I was working another case. But apparently, Nina, the whole thing was pretty cut and dried. Pretty routine. The plane was a Beechcraft 550. That's a dependable private jet with very few problems in its history. It had taken off at eight a.m. as scheduled. Two mechanics had prepped it, two veterans—guys who had never made a mistake, apparently. They testified then, and they still do, that it checked out perfectly."

"This just doesn't make any sense."

"Actually, it makes less and less. There are all kinds of cameras around. Homeland Security, you understand."

"I see."

"There's a film, taken from the control tower, scanning the tarmac and the runway. You can see Thornbloom and his pilot walking toward the plane and getting into it. They're laughing and patting each other on the back. Apparently this has been Thornbloom's regular pilot for years. He's perfect. Never had a complaint, never a problem of any kind. Anyway, each of these guys was carrying a little suitcase and a thermos of coffee. This stuff they took onto the plane with them. The mechanics watched them board the plane. And the mechanics swear, Nina, that nothing else was on the plane. No strange packages, no bombs. Nothing that *could* have been a bomb."

"And yet…"

"Yeah. *And yet.* The plane took off perfectly, the weather stayed perfect, Thornbloom *was on the plane* and two hours later the plane disappeared from radar. Not one word of a problem, just…gone. The Coast Guard found a bit of wreckage three hours later, but the ocean is two miles deep at that point. No bodies, no black box."

"How far out were they?"

"One thousand, two hundred and twenty miles."

"How high were they flying?"

"Forty thousand feet."

"And Thornbloom came in here this morning and left me another dirty letter."

"Well, I wouldn't exactly call it *dirty*."

"Let's not quibble."

"All right. Yes, according to Proctor, he came in here."

"Well, then, we just have to resort to literature."

"That's what we have to do?"

"Yes, that's all that's left. Sherlock Holmes tells us we only have to eliminate the impossible, and believe what's left."

"And when we do that in this case?"

Nina shrugged:

"Thornbloom survived the forty thousand foot crash, got out of the airplane, and swam back to shore."

"Nina, he's seventy-eight years old."

"And I have to say, it's a remarkable achievement for a man of that age."

Sylvia stared at her for a time.

Before she could reply, the door to the office opened.

It was Dicken Proctor.

He still had the same shocked look on his face that Nina had seen the morning before.

There was nothing to be said to him, so the two women simply watched as he sat down in the chair closest to the door.

As though drawn to him by some kind of magnetism, they pulled chairs close by and they themselves sat.

A ring of three people sitting silently in an office that looked like a sideshow booth advertising the Old South.

Finally Nina asked:

"Did they let you go, Dicken?"

A shrug:

"They couldn't really hold me. I haven't done anything wrong."

"Except to see a ghost."

Dicken Proctor shook his head:

"It wasn't a ghost, Nina. It was Thornbloom."

"And this is what you kept telling them?"

"Yes. And they would never believe me. Maybe I don't even believe me. Thornbloom is at the bottom of the ocean. There's no way he could be anywhere else. People—responsible people—saw him get on the airplane, saw the plane take off. The plane remained on the radar screen until it disappeared two hours after take off. It couldn't have turned back."

"And yet..."

"And yet I saw him here in this office, Nina. As clear as anything I've ever seen in my life."

He pressed a palm against his forehead, leaned back in his chair, and breathed deeply. Then he continued:

"I worked with the man for ten years. I was close to him. I made him coffee on the morning he took off in that plane."

"Yes, you told me that."

"I would know him from a mile away. No one looks precisely like him. Six foot two, those blue eyes...I couldn't have been mistaken. Nina..."

"Yes, Dicken?"

"That night in the library. When the man stalked you. You didn't get a glimpse of him, did you? Tall man, silver haired?"

"I'm sorry, Dicken. The stacks were between us. I couldn't see anything at all of him."

"Too bad. If somebody could just corroborate..."

Then, a slow shaking of the head:

"It doesn't matter. I know they're not going to believe me. That's why, when they told me under no circumstances was I to tell this wild story to the press or anyone else...Nina, I decided to hold back one thing. Why tell it to them if they weren't going to believe me anyway?"

She stared at him for a time.

Then:

"What is it, Dicken? What did you hold back?"

"All right. You have a right to know. You were almost killed. If anybody has right to know, it's you."

"Tell me."

"Two nights before the day he…the day…"

"I know. Go on."

"Two nights before, we were up in his office in the Cannon Building. It had been a long day. Lots of visitors, lots of meetings. So now it was late and everybody else had already gone home. Sometimes when that happened—and it happened pretty frequently—he would take out a bottle of brandy that he kept in his desk. We would sip a glass. No more. But a small glass. So this night we'd almost finished it, when he looked at me and said: 'Dicken, I think he's trying to talk to me.' I didn't understand. I asked something like, 'Jarrod'—after we had worked together for years, he began to insist that I call him by his first name—'Jarrod, who is trying to talk to you?'"

"But he just shook his head, as though it should have been self evident. He just shook his head and said: 'He's been coming to me. And talking to me. And he's been telling me that I've been wrong. For all these years, I've been wrong. Like the Apostle Paul, I've been kicking against the pricks. I've been promoting evil causes. Dicken, he's been telling me that I must act. I must wipe out the evil.'"

Dicken Proctor shook his head:

"I didn't know what to say. And that was all he said. Then we finished our brandy, washed out the glasses, put the bottle away, and went home."

"You didn't," Nina asked, "talk about this again the next day?"

A shake of the head:

"No. But Nina, I have to tell you: I think Jarrod Thornbloom is alive. And I think he's gone insane. And

I think he imagines God is talking to him, and telling him…"

"Telling him what?"

"To kill Laurencia Dalrymple. And to kill you."

CHAPTER SIXTEEN: A PHONE CALL AT MIDNIGHT

At first, she did not know what had awakened her.

It might have been the incessant pounding of rain on the window across the bedroom, for the storm had hit shortly before twelve (there had been flashes of lightning and rumblings of thunder at ten-thirty, when she had gone to bed.)

"Laurencia!"

She propped herself up in the bed.

"Laurencia!"

No answer.

She got out of bed, got into her slippers and robe, and wandered dazedly into the kitchen.

"Laurencia?"

Carefully she opened the door to Laurencia's bedroom.

Empty bed.

She was, as she had sensed, alone in the apartment.

"Where is that coming from?"

She returned to her own bedroom and was aware of it for the first time.

Her cell phone was buzzing.

She had set it carefully on the nightstand before she got into bed. Now it glowed blue, buzzed like an adder, and vibrated its way toward the edge of the stand, as though it were trying to escape and get under the bed before it could be captured.

She flipped it open, put it to her cheek, and breathed into it:

"Hello?"

A pause.

Simply the sound of breathing at the other end.

"Hello?"

Then:

"Nina?"

It was…

"Nina?"

"Laurencia!"

"Nina?"

"Where are you? Are you all right?"

Then merely the same pause, the same sound of breathing.

Followed by a low, raspy:

"Hello, Nina. It's nice to talk to you."

She caught her breath.

A flash of lightning illuminated the room.

BAM said the thunder.

FLASH answered more lightning.

"I so enjoyed our time in the library. Didn't you?"

She could not speak.

"Can't you answer me? I've gone to a great deal of trouble to reach you."

And, finally, she could answer.

"Who are you?"

Pause.

Wheezing of breath.

And:

"That's the question, isn't it?"

"What do you want?"

Wheeze.

Wheeze.

Then, quietly:

"Nothing. Any more."

"What are you talking about? How did you get this number?"

"I have access to a great many things. Most of them, as I now realize, useless."

"What have you done with Laurencia?"

"Nothing."

"If you've hurt her..."

"I have not. But it is over now."

"What do you mean? What are you planning to do?"

"End it. The voice tells me to end it. Tonight."

"Listen, you have to..."

"I have to end it. That is all. I obey only the voice. Only the one voice and no other. I have done my best. And now it is time to go."

"Let me talk to Laurencia!"

"Of course. Laurencia is, I'm certain, quite eager to speak with you."

"Then put her on! I want to be sure she's all right!"

"No. You must come here."

The sentence hit her like a blow in the stomach.

For a time she could not speak.

Then:

"What? What did you say?"

"I said that you must come here."

"I...I can't do that."

"And why ever not?"

"I don't know where you are."

"Six eleven Clifford St. It's a lovely garden apartment. Clifford Street is a mile or so above the U Street neighborhood. You'll love it here, Nina. It's a side of Washington that Laurencia and her friends have never shown you. Perhaps, to tell the truth, they've never seen it themselves. And that's such a shame. For this neighborhood never rests. Laurencia and I, as we speak, are watching through the window, and looking at the sidewalk. Only the spattering of rain is to be seen, for the people who live and visit here are all warm and cozy inside the bars and the brothels. But the rain will stop sometime. And then they will be out again. The lovely ladies with their high heels and their red dresses and the long cigarettes that they smoke. All of this world you shall visit tonight. How exciting."

"This apartment is ringed by security people. I can't just get out and go where I want to."

A pause and then the voice became deeper, more menacing:

"Then find a way, dammit! Sneak out in the rain! Whoever's watching that damned place is dozing in the back seat or playing pinochle. And, by the way, aren't you supposed to be the great Nina Bannister? Hell, you and this woman sitting here with me are supposed to be the next leaders of the free world! And you can't get out of your own apartment? Don't make me laugh!"

Another pause, and then the voice regained its earlier icy calmness.

"You're biggest problem, Nina, might be finding a cab that will come here. Most of them won't do so after midnight. Such cowards they all are!"

"Look, if you just…"

"And do be aware: you must come alone."

"I'm just not certain that I…"

"Because if you don't—if you try to bring your beautiful Hispanic Secret Service friend—or any stray policemen you may have picked up—if you do either of those things, I will immediately cut the throat of Ms.— sorry, *Senator*—Dalrymple here."

"Please, please just…"

"Good night, Nina."

And he hung up.

For a time, she simply sat on the side of the bed, thinking, hearing the bellowing of the storm and having no idea what to do.

Was this Jarrod Thornbloom, having ultimately gone mad?

Dicken had been certain.

Dicken had worked with Thornbloom for ten years. And Dicken was certain.

And as for Laurencia—how had he managed to abduct her? What had happened to *her* security?

And yet she could not forget the voice.

"Nina?"

"Nina?"

Exactly how Laurencia always sounded on the phone.

'You have to come.'

'Six eleven Clifford St.'

She sat and thought.

The security people were down there.

She could call them immediately.

She could call Sylvia Morales.

And, oh, how she wanted to do that!

Within ten minutes, perhaps less, there would be policemen and women swarming all over this lunatic's *garden* apartment (if such a place even existed).

They would go in and find him and capture him.

And it would all be over.

She paused.

And, her thought continued on its own, like a runaway train, and Laurencia would be found lying in the bed with her throat cut.

No.

No, she had to go.

Dr. King's words came back to her:

"The ultimate measure of a—woman—is not where— —she—stands in moments of convenience and comfort, but where she stands at times of challenge and controversy."

Well.

A little controversy here.

And a little challenge.

She got off the bed and began to get dressed.

Doing this took some time and also took her into Laurencia's bedroom, where she found in one of the closets a massive dark green rain slicker—her own was still in Bay St. Lucy—and equally formidable galoshes. In ten minutes time, she was outfitted like a forest ranger with everything but hatchet and hose. In twelve minutes' time, she was furtively shoving open the back porch door, much as Furl had learned to nose open her front porch door when he sensed food on the landing.

The rain was pouring harder than ever now, rattling on the paving stones beneath, and falling in sheets so thick that nothing could be seen from more than ten feet away except for the faint blue of street lights, which looked like stars twinkling oh-so-faintly in a water sky.

She made her way down the rickety back stairway, feeling like a burglar in reverse.

She reached the bottom stair and turned right, up the sidewalk, heading East.

Were those cars parked a few feet away or just inert blobs of metal with streams of water running off their useless hoods?

Hard to tell.

At any rate, she realized that, if she could see nothing, than neither could she be seen.

She splashed her way on, up the street.

One of the finest law enforcement agencies in the world was now attempting to protect her.

And she was doing her best to escape from it.

In five minutes she *had* escaped from it.

And in ten minutes, feeling surprisingly warm due to the quality of Laurencia's rain gear—she felt as though she were standing in a diving bell—she was standing at the northwest corner of Mt. Vernon Square.

"Taxi!"

There were several, even at midnight, even in this storm.

One of them pulled over and stopped.

She bent down and shouted through a crack in the open window:

"Six eleven Clifford Street! It's…"

"I know where it is," said the driver, and pulled away.

This happened twice more.

Finally, she found a driver who would take her.

She clambered into the cab, feeling like an otter.

"Sorry," she panted, wiping rainwater out of her eye and giving up on the prospect of ever drying her hair, "about getting your backseat wet."

The driver pulled into the street, but looked at her through the mirror:

"You sure you give me the right address?"

"Yes."

"You know somebody up there?"

Pause.

"Yes," she lied.

"It's good you know somebody up there, 'cause— well, when I let you out, I'd like to see you meet somebody you know."

"It will be okay."

"Lot of guys won't go up there. Lot of robberies happen up there."

"If you want more money…"

A shake of the driver's head:

"Naw. I just want to be sure you're safe. Want to be certain you know somebody up in that neighborhood."

"I do," she said for the third time.

Then she simply pressed her nose against the window, and watched Washington flow past.

Leaving Mr. Vernon Square, they drove north on 7th St., through a neighborhood where the two Starbucks on each block had just closed; through a seedier neighborhood that housed only one Starbucks per block (that one having closed hours earlier in the evening), into a neighborhood with only nondescript coffee shops, into a neighborhood of taverns, into a neighborhood of bars, and finally into a neighborhood of brothels.

The rain continued to pour down.

Through garishly open windows she could see people drinking and playing pool. Outside, between the drinking establishments and below seedy hotel windows, women dressed in colored underwear and foot-tall high heels were huddled back into alleys, points of fire designating the middle of their lips.

Nina paid the driver, opened the door, and got out, putting her rain boot squarely in a six-inch puddle.

"Who you know up here?" asked the driver.

She had to shout to make herself heard over the rattling of the rain on the cab, and over the sounds of music wailing, pool balls clicking, big men cursing, and bigger men replying, that were oozing out into the street around her.

"My aunt."

"Your what?"

"My aunt lives up here."

The driver shook his head:

"You've got some aunt."

Nina nodded:

"Yes. She's a tough old bird."

"Good luck to her. And good luck to you."

"Thank you."

"Six eleven is right over there."

And so saying, the cab driver pulled away.

Leaving her in the middle of the toughest neighborhood she had ever seen, except when she visited Tom Broussard.

She breathed deeply, and the rain pelted her.

This was insane.

Nothing was to keep this man from killing her, from killing both of them.

But if she turned now and ran away, simply ran until she had covered the five or ten or fifteen blocks where Starbucks again thrived and cabs still prowled—if she did this, she could be back home under her own sheets within an hour.

And Laurencia would almost certainly be dead, lying in a seedy apartment bed with her throat cut.

So she turned and walked toward a metal railing on the sidewalk, beyond which was a lighted window, beside which was a darkened five-foot flight of descending stairs.

Ending in a doorway.

Above which had been nailed the dingy gray numbers *six eleven*.

The window glowed yellow, but it was so dirty that she could make out nothing inside.

"Okay. Let's get this over with."

She walked down the stairs.

The heavy wooden door confronted her.

There was a button of some kind on the wall just beside the handle.

She pressed it. A buzzing sound could be heard from within.

But nothing seemed to move.

She knocked on the door.

Again, nothing.

Summoning all her courage, she found that she was able to shout:

"Laurencia!"

The thunder rumbled in answer and the lightning flashed and the rain deluged and a rat ran across the ground between her feet and the door stop.

But nothing else.

So she turned the door knob and pressed.

The door swung open.

Before her loomed a lighted, narrow hallway, with a single light bulb hanging from the ceiling, held up by a frayed cord.

"Laurencia?"

She stepped forward.

No reply.

She walked on.

Then she looked left.

The apartment, she could see, consisted only of one room, with a bathroom tucked into one corner and the semblance of a kitchen tucked into another.

On the far side, through the window, she could see rain pellets spattering off the sidewalk.

Then she looked at the walls.

They were covered with signs, made out of butcher paper and carrying messages scrawled in red, blue, or black markers:

GOD IS COMING!

HOMOSEXUALITY IS BESTIAL!

ABORTIONISTS WILL FRY IN HELL!

WOMEN—KNOW YOUR MASTERS!

There, just to her left, in the center of the room, was a stack of envelopes, and beside it a few sheets of stationery.

Cream colored.

And just beyond that was the single bed.

And on it, lay a body.

Despite herself, and knowing somehow, seeing the lifeless blue eyes fixed unseeingly on a spot in the ceiling, the hand hanging never again to be moved over the bedside, the fingertips reaching almost to faded carpet—knowing of course that she had nothing to fear from this figure, she made her way across the room and peered down into the corpse's face.

Straggled white hair, still ruddy complexion...

Baggy, formless slacks, white shirt, now stained...

...those eyes, staring upward.

"*That*," she whispered to herself, the words floating down to ears that could not hear, "is Jarrod Thornbloom."

CHAPTER SEVENTEEN: WHERE ONE GOES IN OUR NATION'S CAPITAL WHEN IT IS VERY LATE AT NIGHT AND ALL OF THE STARBUCKS ARE CLOSED

They all went to the headquarters of the Secret Service.

Sylvia was there.

Laurencia had been brought there.

Dicken Proctor had been brought there.

Jeb Maxwell, the House Majority Whip had been brought there.

Nina was there.

And Stockmeyer, Head of the Secret Service, had just strode into the room.

He looked around the table where they all were sitting and said:

"It's not Thornbloom."

No one spoke.

Stockbridge continued:

"It's a dead ringer for the man. Six foot two, white beard, blue eyes, same facial structure...but it's not Thornbloom."

Silence.

Finally, Nina:

"I'm sorry that I said it was. I had never seen Jarrod Thornbloom. Only pictures of him, and, of course, only on TV."

Stockbridge merely nodded:

"That's all right. The resemblance is remarkable."

Dicken Proctor:

"You're sure it's not him?"

"We're sure. Fingerprints."

"Well. Now that I think back upon that morning in the office. The sun had not come up. The lights were dimmed."

"You made a mistake. It happens. And you, Congresswoman Bannister, made an even bigger mistake."

Nina nodded, knowing what was sure to come.

"I know. I'm sorry."

"You went up there by yourself."

"Yes."

"What in God's name were you thinking?"

"He had Laurencia. He said he was going to kill her."

But Laurencia merely leaned forward and said:

"I was on the Hill, dear. We had an emergency meeting in response to a bill that is to come up tomorrow. These things happen frequently."

"I heard you. I heard your voice on the phone."

No one spoke.

Finally Stockmeyer:

"I'm not sure how that is possible. I'm also not sure how this man was able to get your number."

"But who," asked Nina, "is the man, anyway?"

A shrug of Stockmeyer's shoulders:

"We were able to identify him a little over an hour ago. I could give you a name, but it wouldn't matter. He's a small time crook and drug dealer. The city's full of them. Quite a few arrests."

"How did he die?"

"Drug overdose. Heroin."

"He said," Nina said quietly, "that the voices had told him to end it."

Sylvia Morales spoke up.

"All we can figure, Nina, is that this guy went from penny-ante drug pushing to crazed social activism."

"Or just insanity."

"Maybe it was that. Maybe the drugs had something to do with it. But whatever caused it, he was clearly the nut who was writing you all those letters, and the nut who stalked you to the library, and the nut who shot at you."

Silence for a time.

Finally, Dicken Proctor, quietly:

"Well, I'm sorry he did it, and I'm sorry he's dead. I also realize this means Jarrod is where we thought he was, at the bottom of the sea. But it means too, that there are no ghosts walking around, and that I'm not insane."

Stockmeyer:

"No, Mr. Proctor; you aren't insane. And maybe, maybe, this nightmare is over for all of you."

"Will we still need protection?" asked Nina.

Stockmeyer nodded:

"There are still a lot of crazies out there, and this Lissie movement is getting more and more controversial as the 4th of July approaches. I understand you're going to be flying to Bay St. Lucy—along with Laurencia and you, Mr. Proctor—for the theatrical production?"

"For *Lysistrata*, yes."

"Well, Sylvia will be going along, and we'll have some other folks there who we're coordinating with in the Mississippi branch. Don't run away from them, all right?"

"I'm sorry about that."

"We can't help you if you don't work with us."

"I understand."

Smiles all around.

And somehow, Nina began to realize, there should have been smiles all around.

She was crazy.

She had done a stupid thing.

If the voices had told the lunatic not to kill himself with a drug overdose, but to kill her…

…but that did not happen.

And now she was all right.

She was going home.

To Margot.

To Alanna.

To Jackson.

To her little shack.

And to Furl.

She was going home, and the danger was over.

These things she told herself.

And these things—all of them—were completely wrong.

CHAPTER EIGHTEEN: RESPECT!

The strains of Aretha Franklin's music wafted over them as they exited the plane at Bay St. Lucy Regional Airport.

This was only a coincidence. The giant speakers that had been erected just outside the airport entrance gates were playing Aretha Franklin at the moment; but they could play any of a number of other songs that had been blaring into the balmy wet summer air for the last few days, or since the beginning of the week leading to July 4.

They could have been playing:

Mavis Staples, "A Change is Gonna Come!"

or...

Katie Perry, "Roar!"

or...

K.D. Lang, "Hallelujah!"

or...

Helen Reddy, "I am Woman, Hear Me Roar!"

or...

Carol King, "You've Got a Friend!"

Or any of a seemingly endless chain of songs about strength and sisterhood and power and WOMEN WOMEN WOMEN sung by WOMEN WOMEN WOMEN to WOMEN WOMEN WOMEN who had decided they had HAD ENOUGH and now wished TO TAKE NO MORE!

But these were only words.

More important, by far, were the sights and sounds that were now deluging the entire stretch of coast in which nature had chosen to embed little Bay St. Lucy.

Boats, ships, a floating armada of colors and sails and mastheads and flags dotted the sea for at least two miles out, and Nina had been astonished at their number, at their variety.

The door to the cockpit had opened some moments before they were actually to land, and the captain, smiling, had stuck his head back into the cabin:

"We're cleared to land if we want to, but I thought you might want to circle the city at least once. There's some amazing things going on down there!"

"Do it!" shouted Laurencia, who was seated next to Nina, and adjacent to the window.

"Yes, do it!" echoed Dicken Proctor, from two rows further back. "This is what we've come to see!"

"All right! Hold onto your hats!"

So they began to circle.

The town itself had been engulfed with mobs of people, who milled and danced and swam and sunned and shouted and pointed up at the plane, shouting and waving signs.

But all of these people were nothing compared to the massive mob that had packed itself into the Bay St. Lucy football stadium, which could hold at a maximum two thousand football fans, who, even at their most excited, could hardly hope to reach the fervor being shown by the immense crowd down below, a crowd packed as thickly as human bodies could allow themselves to be, and singing along deliriously as a woman played keyboard on a huge stage that had been erected in the middle of the field. The woman was backed by two guitarists. The drummer was going crazy as all good drummers do, and the bass player could be seen, even five-hundred feet below, to be in a world of his own.

They were all in a world of their own.

Bay St. Lucy had gone crazy, had eaten its fill of the psychedelic mushroom that animated and drove the soul of the feminine life force.

The woman was dressed all in red, with an even redder scarf; and as the plane circled lower, she looked up at it, perhaps recognized whom it might be carrying—then stood up, jumped away from the keyboard, and ripped off her jacket.

To reveal, of course, a black *Lissie* t-shirt.

She pumped her arm, raised her hands, and bellowed at the sky.

The crowd, which had gone mad some time ago, went madder.

Huge screens that had been erected where the goal posts should have been, flashed the words of the song the woman was singing.

"Who is that?" asked Nina.

Laurencia turned and stared at her:

"What?"

"Who is that? On the stage. Singing."

"I can't believe you're asking me that."

"Well. I don't know."

"Baby, where have you been all your life?"

"Teaching high school."

"Even so…"

"Humor me, Laurencia."

"That is Annie Lennox, dear.

"Look at that mob," said Nina, still stunned.

"Well, you started it."

Nina shook her head.

"Maybe. Maybe that *no* I said was the spark. But it was all pent up and ready to go. There were fifty million gallons of woman explosives. I just set off the bomb."

And the bomb she had set off had transformed Bay St. Lucy.

If not the entire country.

If not the entire world.

Still, though, flooded with journalists and cameras and reporters and protesters and demonstrators and Gay Rights advocates and Abortion Rights advocates and Environmental Protection advocates and Rock Music advocates and Rap Music advocates and Animal Protection Rights advocates and Tea Party advocates and Down With the Tea Party advocates and thousands and thousands and thousands of conscientious voters and good citizens and concerned men and women and just plain idiots—

—though flooded with all these idiots, Bay St. Lucy was still home.

The air felt of home as it moved around her, warm and sultry and salt-sticky—as she descended the ramp and put her shoes on the tarmac.

Nina Bannister, who had gone off to Washington D.C. and started a revolution, was back where she had come from.

All her friends were there to meet her, of course.

Margot had driven down from The Candles, and embraced her, and cried on the top of her head.

Alanna Delafosse, several inches shorter, cried on her cheek.

Jackson, several hundred pounds bigger, picked her up and looked at her and grinned and shook her a few times and set her gently on the earth, aware of how breakable she was.

Macy Cox embraced her as heartily as any of the others, and would have cried on her, but was still too happy in her marriage to be able to cry, even tears of happiness, and so just smiled and told her how proud she was, how proud the whole town was.

About fifty yards from the airplane, a small brass band from the high school began to play, and the crowd of fifty or so Bay St. Lucyans that had come to meet the plane attempted to sing:
CHEER CHEER CHEER
FOR THE WOMAN OF THE YEAR
(I TELL YOU)
CHEER CHEER CHEER
FOR THE WOMAN OF THE YEAR
...while waving signs showing Nina's face and Laurencia's face.

But this band could hardly be heard over the gigantic loud speakers—four of them that had been planted like massive refrigerators at twenty-five yard intervals along the side of the runway—which continued to channel Aretha, who was now bellowing her famous lyrics, asking for—no—demanding—respect...

...which she was, Nina found herself musing, almost certain to be granted.

All of the introductory formalities, the social fusion of the nation's capital and Mississippi's CUTE CRAFTS AND POTS capital, lasted for a little more than an hour.

But finally it was done, for at least a short time. The photographs were made; the brief statements to various newspapers were spoken; a million smiles were beamed out; the DC delegation, Laurencia chief among them, but several other Representatives and two Senators, plus various and sundry staffers—Dicken Proctor being one of them—were taken by limousines to the new high-rise Nina Bannister High School, where they ascended to the fourth floor and looked out the window of the principal's office, down onto the floor of the now emptying stadium—then to the wharf area, where power boats were to whisk them out to a gigantic luxury vessel—provided, of course, by Gulf Coast Petroleum, where they were to be housed for the next two days.

And Nina was returned to her shack.

It had, of course, been cordoned off, to protect it from, in the words of Moon Rivard, "a slew of rubberneckers."

But it was the same.

And, as Jackson Bennett eased his big black car to a stop and she felt the oyster shells of the driveway beneath her shoe soles, she exulted at the thought of walking up the familiar rickety staircase...

...which she did...

...and putting her key in the lock...

...which she did...

...and turning it, and hearing the familiar *click*...

...which she did...

...and pushing the door open...

...which she did.

And seeing her living room.

With the kitchen beyond, and beyond that, the deck, and beyond that, the magnificent Gulf of Mexico.

A smile from Jackson.

Then:

"I can't tell you how proud we all are of you, Nina. But we're also glad you're okay. I don't know how much you're allowed to talk about it, but the story is that the nut who shot at you is dead."

"Yes. It seems that way."

"Who was he, Nina? Details are so sketchy..."

She shrugged:

"We don't know a great deal, Jackson. He was a drug addict who somehow snapped. He apparently—at least according to his letters—thought he was hearing the voice of God, which was telling him that women were not supposed to be in power. Finally, he thought that voice was telling him that he should put an end to himself. So, he took a fatal drug overdose. He called me just before he died. I was the one who found the body."

"My God."

"One of the things that made the whole thing worse was that he looked like Thornbloom. Big guy, silver haired, blue eyes. Stockmeyer, who is head of the Secret Service, thinks that he may have played upon that fact to gain entrance to various offices. Somehow he had my telephone number. We may never know how he did that. At any rate, his old Chief of Staff, Dicken Proctor, actually saw him leaving a letter in my office. Poor Dicken thought he had seen a ghost."

"It's incredible."

"The good thing now is, it's over. We can think about tomorrow."

"Yes, we can. The biggest Fourth of July in the history of this town. Or maybe the country. Have you been keeping up with the races?"

She shook her head.

"Not as closely as I would like. I knew pretty well how we stood until day before yesterday. But with all the trip planning…"

Jackson nodded:

"I understand. That's why I brought a list. Thought you might like to see it."

"I do. Where are we?"

"The names of thirty-seven new women candidates have been put on ballots across the country. Some are Democrats, some are Republicans, some have gotten on as third party—Lissie Party—candidates. All have been put there as a result of referenda, mostly spurred on by petition drives run by Lissie Movement agitators. It's amazing. Nothing like this has ever happened. Ever."

"The goal is forty, though. Or it's slumber party time."

Jackson nodded:

"Well, the gym is ready. It's been filled with pallets. I can't say the Bay St. Lucy husbands are all that thrilled."

"It's like Laurencia said. They get a poker night."

Jackson pursed his lips and said:

"They may not need to. Three more referenda are scheduled tomorrow: in Arizona, Wyoming, and Missouri. If the women candidates in those states can make it onto the ballot.."

"..It will be forty-one. And everyone in the country will...well, let's say a lot of babies might wind up being born nine months and one day from today."

Nina looked at the list she had been given:

Mary Hall: North Carolina

Janice Wright: Ohio

Susan Booth: Rhode Island

Sue Robel: Alabama

Gail Hill: Maine

Susan Johnson: Delaware

Catherine McEnroe: Michigan

Angela Granese: Florida

Cindy Barber: West Virginia

Nancy Moore: Kansas

Kathy Berg: Texas

Anna Jenson: Iowa

Holly Damico: Idaho

Sharon Mankey: Indiana

Joanna Blousser: Alaska

Patricia Rockwell: Illinois

Sally Carpenter: California

Liz John: New Jersey

Dreama Reed: Oregon

Jennifer Vido: Maryland

Lynn Boling: Georgia
Melissa Britton: Arkansas
Davida Weaver: Ohio
Sally Carpenter: California
Edwina Teach: Massachusetts
Julie Seedorf: Minnesota
Kay Reidel: Louisiana
Lana Star: Virginia
Deb Hawkins: Utah
Anne Dewell: Mississippi
Kate Reese: Pennsylvania
Sharon Collender: South Carolina
Anna Souchek: North Dakota
Margaret Verhoef: Kansas
May Moore: Wyoming
Nanci Rathbun: Wisconsin
Carrie Kucher: Illinois
Alice Mendez: New Mexico
Jill Pranger: Tennessee
Terri Star: Arizona
Kay Johnson: New Hampshire
Lynn Jones: South Dakota
Georgia Malendraka: New York
Gail Douthat: Vermont

She put the list down, then said:

"Thirty-eight women; thirty-eight states. Can these women be elected in November, Jackson?"

He shrugged:

"I never thought they'd get on ballots. The world has gone crazy."

"Or maybe," Nina said, "it's beginning to go sane. For the first time."

The afternoon was delicious. The little corner of the beach/universe where her shack rested was, she decided, the only part of Bay St. Lucy to offer a bit of peace and quiet, and she made the most of it. She spent it reading *The Murder at the Vicarage* and enjoying the Agatha Christiness that was seeping into her welcoming brain.

The upshot of it all was that she was rested and ready for the gala at the Auberge des Arts, and just as rested and ready to hear Helen Reddington speak to the media about the upcoming *Lysistrata* production, which promised to have—at least in terms of money spent and logistical maneuvers utilized—the scope and dramatic potential of World War II.

The first part of the evening was wonderful, of course, having been planned by Alanna Delafosse and Helen Reddington. There was champagne and more champagne; there was schmoozing beneath the magnificent oaks on the magnificent grounds of the Old Robinson Mansion, where gangsters once roamed and politicians now roamed, neither the foliage in the trees nor the flowers in the gardens nor the glass in the dormer windows nor the full moon in the sky able to tell the difference...

And there were the memorable moments of fusion between Nina's old world of home and her new world of D.C., moments such as the one that saw Alanna and Laurencia meet, embrace, and recognize the kinship that had grown between them for both of their entire lives, without either of them having known for one moment of the other's existence.

Nina would never forget the moment when Laurencia, seated exquisitely within the exquisite gazebo, leaned forward and said quietly to Alanna:

"I will, my sister, be elected."

And Alanna:

"I know that. I know it with all of my heart."

"And I will be needing a Minister of Cultural Affairs."

"I was not aware that such an office existed."

"It did not. Until I saw you, Alanna. At that moment, it came into being. If you would consent to take the job."

And then two wonderful smiles met precisely a foot and a half in front of each woman's mouth, and a small portion of the metal table between them melted.

Nor was the second half of the evening any less fulfilling.

For there was Helen Reddington, beautiful and dark-eyed Helen, who would in only a few short hours become the woman who ended, at least literarily if not historically, the terrible Peloponnesian War, standing at a podium, talking to a room full of reporters about what was to transpire the next evening.

"There is a world of difference," she was saying, "between Old Comedy and New Comedy. New Comedy is Menander, and then, in Rome, Terence. It's sit-com stuff. The beautiful young woman and handsome young man who want to be married, and the ridiculous father who's a miser or a hypochondriac or whatever, and who blocks them. Every one of our thirty-minute TV comedy series, from Lucy to Archie Bunker to Burns and Allen to Seinfeld is based on them somehow.

But Old Comedy—Aristophanes' comedy—is completely different. It's wild. It turns universes upside down. It creates Cloud-cuckoo-land. People hang fifty feet above the stage in balloons. Old Comedy is what *Lysistrata* is, and it's what we're going to do here tomorrow night. But not just here. Not just in the Auberge itself. No, a lot of the speaking scenes will be done up on the roof garden, where a good many of the cameras are.

But this production is going to utilize the whole town of Bay St. Lucy, and a stretch of beach at least a mile and a half long. It's going to be epic, and, I promise all of you, unforgettable. Just like the *Lissie* movement is unforgettable. Let me try to make this as clear as I can: when we think today of 'Greek Tragedy,' we think of boring choruses of twelve old men in black robes chanting something. But that wasn't what the real choruses must have been like, it couldn't have been. The real choruses—well, wealthy people spent months putting them together and training them. There was wild music and dancing—and we've lost whatever records may ever have described them. We have no idea what they must have been.

Still, we're going to recreate them tomorrow night. There are going to be choruses all over the city tomorrow night, all dancing to rock music and country western music and African music and—and all the music of the world! These choruses will have one thing in common: they'll all be making their way to the Acropolis, which, of course, is our football stadium. At precisely ten o'clock, Lysistrata will announce from our rooftop here that the Spartans and the Athenians have made peace, and that the Peloponnesian War is over. And at just that moment, a helicopter will land in the middle of our football field. Laurencia Dalrymple will get out of it, and walk to the stage where the fantastic Annie Lennox concert took place today. There she will make the announcement: either forty new women candidates have made it to the ballots for the November election—or they haven't. I'm sure you know that three referenda are taking place tomorrow. It's going to be close. Either way, sex strike or orgy, this *Lysistrata* is going to have one hell of an ending."

CHAPTER NINETEEN: WHAT THE PICTURE SHOWED

It was as though a virus had been injected into Nina Bannister.

Two hours before the massive festivities—arrival of ships, beginning of dancing and singing, beginning of the *Lysistrata* production itself—were to begin.

But by then the virus had begun to work.

Working.

Working.

She had one more interview scheduled for five o'clock.

Just before lunch, she called the appropriate people and cancelled it.

She would have walked along the beach, but she could not do so, because there was no beach. There was just a mob of people.

So she simply went home.

She turned off her cell phone, which had been buzzing like a small blue plastic glowing hornet's nest.

And she paced.

She paced in the living room.

She made herself a sandwich in the kitchen.

She ate it.

She walked out on the deck, watched the marvelous array of ships that were out on the ocean awaiting tonight's spectacle.

Tonight's spectacle.

Which was going to be wonderful, unforgettable.

Except…

…except for the 'something's not quite right here' virus.

Then, sitting on the deck, she herself began to hear voices.

That same voice, actually.

The one that came to her as the voice of God must have come to the lunatic who tried to kill her.

"Hello Jane," she found herself whispering to the deck rail. "Hello, Jane Austen."

"A mind lively and at ease, Nina."

"Yes, I know."

" A mind lively and at ease, can do with seeing nothing, and can see nothing that does not answer."

All right, Nina Bannister…

…think.

Your mind is lively, and always has been.

Just don't let it be at ease.

Don't let it be at ease.

What's wrong?

What doesn't fit?

What…

And then she saw it.

"No," she whispered to herself. "No, it's not possible."

And it wasn't.

It couldn't have been.

So thinking, she walked into her living room, turned on the cell phone, and made a call.

Ten minutes later, Sylvia Morales, dressed casually in dungarees and a Janice Joplin sweatshirt, was knocking at her door.

"Nina?"

She crossed the living room, opened the door, and immediately felt a sense of relief.

Sylvia.

Sylvia instilled confidence.

That quiet smile, those dark eyes.

"Nina, what is it?"

She shook her head:

"I don't know, Sylvia."

"Has something happened? I thought you'd be at the Auberge getting ready to watch the play."

"No, I… it's just…"

"What?"

"Something I thought of. Something that isn't right, Sylvia."

"I don't know what you're talking about. There are agents scattered everywhere around town. The FBI, the state police, the local guys—there must be a hundred people in Bay St. Lucy. And, I've got to tell you, it's a pretty good crowd. Hardly any incidents to talk about, if you don't count the marijuana, which we're ignoring. No, otherwise, it's just pretty festive."

"I'm glad to hear that. But something's wrong. Something just doesn't fit."

"What?"

"Sylvia, do you remember the pictures?"

"What pictures?"

"The ones taken at Dulles Airport."

"Showing Thornbloom and his pilot?"

"Yes, those pictures."

"Sure, I remember them."

"I want to see them."

"Why?"

"Just—one detail."

"I don't know what you're talking about."

"Maybe I'm not talking about anything. But I need to see those pictures."

"Well, I've got Stockmeyer's private number."

"Can he get them to you?"

A nod.

"Sure. He can email them to me on my smart phone. That's done pretty frequently."

"Then please, call him."

"What am I going to give him for a reason?"

"Tell him Nina Bannister likes to look at airports."

"I'm not sure that will do. But I can tell him there are a couple of loose ends that I would like to tie up. I can also tell him to contact the President of the United States if he has any questions."

Sylvia made the call.

Stockmeyer was not immediately available.

The two women went outside to the deck to wait.

There, half a mile out, were Nina's favorite two porpoises, leaping, making their way west toward Port Aransas.

They had always, she found herself thinking, betokened good luck.

She needed good luck now.

And so, if her suspicions were right, did Laurencia Dalrymple.

It took an hour and a half for Sylvia's phone to buzz.

During that time, marvelous things had begun to happen.

Ships—small ships, large ships, boats, barges, floats, and every imaginable form of nautical transportation, began to make their way toward Bay St. Lucy's beachfront, and these vessels disgorged landing craft, as though the invasion of Normandy beachhead were being reenacted.

Except that these were not soldiers.

These were WOMEN WOMEN WOMEN from not only every state in the union but also seemingly every country in the world.

Here, landing here, a boat filled with Senegalese women, splendidly arrayed in gold and black robes, a huge radio blasting drumbeats as, splashing their way onto the shore and laughing wildly, they began dancing across the sand and up onto the sidewalk that once had taken tourists toward downtown, and that now was taking half of the world's female population toward a one-time football stadium.

And there! Another craft filled with Asian women wearing kimonos.

All forming choruses.

All dancing.

As the moon rose.

And Bay St. Lucy's bacchanal began!

"Has he sent it?"

Sylvia nodded, and handed the smart phone to Nina.

"Here's the picture. There's nothing in it we didn't already know about."

"I'm not so sure of that. Here, let me see."

"Take it."

Nina did, and she looked at it again.

Only this time she looked at it with Jane Austen.

'Can do with seeing nothing…'

See the whole picture Nina.

See the *whole picture*!

"Yes. Yes!"

"What? What are you talking about?"

"They've each got one. That's how he did it!"

"How who did what?"

"He's going to kill Laurencia, Sylvia. It's all worked out just as he planned it. And tonight, somehow, some way, he's going to kill Laurencia."

And at precisely that moment, even though she had no way of knowing it, the play *Lysistrata* began on the rooftop of the Auberge des Arts.

And all of Bay St. Lucy saw on huge screens what all of the nation and the world saw on mobile apps and, for the very old and infirm, TV screens. Helen

Reddington strode forth in her white Athenian robes and met the women from Sparta and Delos and Thebes and Corinth—and told them about the sex strike that would spread across Greece and last until the horrible war between Athens and Sparta would end, and the people would dance in jubilation.

Nina and Sylvia were heading to the airport.

It might happen there.

Sylvia was on her two-way radio.

"Put me through to the tower!"

Pause.

And during that interminable pause, the women of Greece were taking their oath:

NO LOVER AND NO HUSBAND AND NO MAN ON EARTH

SHALL ERE APPROACH ME WITH HIS PENIS UP

AND I SHALL LEAD AN UNLAID LIFE ALONE AT HOME

WEARING A SAFFRON GOWN AND GROOMED AND BEAUTIFIED

SO THAT MY HUSBAND WILL BE ALL ON FIRE FOR ME

BUT I WILL NEVER WILLINGLY GIVE IN TO HIM

AND IF HE TRIES TO FORCE ME TO AGAINST MY WILL

I'LL DO IT BADLY AND NOT WIGGLE IN RESPONSE

NOR POINT THE TOES OF MY BEAUTIFUL SHOES TOWARD THE CEILING

NOR CROUCH UPON HIM IN THE HUNGRY LION POSITION

Nor could Nina know that the oath takers—Kalonika and Lampito and Myrrhina and the others—were solemnizing their vows with mutual drinks from the overflowing wine bowl, while Sylvia was shouting into the phone:

"Stop the helicopter! Stop the copter that's going to take Senator Dalrymple to the football stadium. You've got to...damn!"

"What, Sylvia?"

"The helicopter just took off!"

"But Laurencia's not scheduled to speak until the play is over. And that won't be for another hour, anyway!"

"Laurencia asked them to take off early. She wants to see all the choruses making their way through town."

"Can you contact the helicopter pilot?"

"And tell him what? Nina, what the hell is going on?"

"I just...I can't...I just have this feeling!"

"*What* feeling? I'm just one little agent, Nina—I can't order the next President of the United States around because you've got a feeling."

"All right, then come on."

"Where are we going?"

"To the center of the world; the Acropolis."

And they did.

Or at least they tried to.

It was not easy making one's way through Bay St. Lucy, where all traffic had been banned, and where people of all sizes and shapes and colors and degrees of sobriety were packed together like grains of sand on a flooded beach, if grains of sand on a flooded beach could ever be imagined planning a sand/sex strike if denied sand/gender equity.

They moved slowly.

They could, of course, call any of the two hundred or so agents scattered through the town.

But what would they tell them?

That Nina had a *feeling*?

Nina herself did not know much more than that.

And so they made the Stink Shoppe and Crafts by Laura, where people were buying everything in sight, and where store owner after store owner were saying quietly and to themselves THANK YOU NINA THANK YOU NINA THANK YOU NINA! for making me rich.

And, yes, they did make their way along, glancing also upward at the nearest huge screen where the play had progressed mightily, so that overhead cameras carried by a bright red helicopter were now picturing the Chorus of Old Men being routed by the Chorus of Young Women, a confrontation that took place in Gerard Park, and that ended with the victorious women taking from the men and throwing away, the rotted logs which had served as scatological imagery, being held dragging in front of them as the chorus men had been trained to do.

VICTORY FOR THE WOMEN!

Shouts everywhere, and arms upraised, and HAIL TO THE LISSIES being sung all over town.

And still they made their way along.

Finally, it loomed before them.

The stadium, lights glowing as if this were Friday night and Hattiesburg was in town to take on the Mariners.

"What are we looking for, Nina?"

"I don't know exactly. I don't know how he would do it, but…"

See the whole picture, Nina.

See the…

"Yes! Yes, that's how he would do it!"

"What are you talking about?"

"I'm a principal. We have to go to my office. But not my office. The new principal's office!"

"Are you crazy?"

But Nina simply pointed.

Up.

At the new high rise building that was Bay St. Lucy High School.

That had just opened a month ago.

And that towered over the football stadium.

The building she had toured yesterday, shortly upon her arrival.

The building that had seemed completely safe to her. Then.

Sylvia saw it too, saw all of the windows, and said, quietly:

"I'm making the same mistake. A rookie's mistake. That's the high ground. It's just like the office building that guy shot you from."

"Yes, it is."

"But that guy is dead!"

"No he isn't. *A* guy is dead. But not *that* guy! Not *our* guy! Listen, Sylvia, can you call Moon Rivard?"

'Sure. I can call anybody!"

"Do it, call them all! Tell as many men as possible to meet us at the main door of the high school! But we've got to be sure Moon's there, because he'll have a key to get us in!"

Sylvia made the calls.

It took them almost five minutes to reach the building.

Just before they did so:

"Look!" said Sylvia, pointing upward.

"Damn!"

A helicopter was circling the stadium.

The same bus-like cream-colored helicopter that had taken Nina to the Aquatica

The helicopter that was carrying Laurencia,

Moon stepped forward:

"Nina Bannister! The most famous woman we got, or ever had!"

"Moon, open the door!"

"What's the trouble?"

"I think that…I'm sorry I can't explain right now. Somebody said something he couldn't know. And Laurencia's landing now, and…dammit, just open the door!"

He did so, and Nina was the first one through it..

"Nina!" several voices echoed behind her, "stop! Don't go up there!"

But she was already in the stairwell.

It was the library in reverse.

Then she was being chased down stairs.

The prey.

Now she was racing upstairs.

The hunter.

Even through the thick walls of the building she could hear massive cheering.

The helicopter must have landed.

Laurencia must be getting out of it.

Walking toward the stage.

"Don't let me be too late!" she hissed to herself.

And, as she was doing so, all of the choruses that had now made their way to the Acropolis/Stadium were singing as one—for Lysistrata the Athenian and Lampito the Spartan and Kalonike the Dorian and Myrrihna the Corinthian—had ended the war, the ruinous war, the cataclysmic war—

—and they were now chanting in exultation:

ALAILAI!

BOUND AND LEAP HIGH! ALAILAI!

CRY AS FOR VICTORY!

ALAILAI!

With the last ALAILAI, Nina had opened the door into the fourth floor corridor.

The principal's office...

...to the right!

Don't let me be too late, don't let me be too late, don't let me be too late...

She hurtled down the hall with Moon, Sylvia and the others now close behind...

There was the door...

She reached forward and shoved with all her might.

It swung open.

And there he was, on the other side of the room, his deer rifle propped on the window sill.

Just as he had planned to do the previous day, when he had visited this office with Nina.

And had seen the perfect view of the stage that had been constructed.

He turned.

There was complete silence for an instant.

Then Nina:

"Dicken! Dicken, don't!"

He shook his head:

"I have no choice. The voice..."

"There is no voice, Dicken. It's all in your head. It always has been."

"I've got to kill her. She's evil."

"No, she isn't, Dicken. No one is evil. You have to get help now."

He shook his head:

"There is no help for me. There can never be. But how did you know?"

"It didn't fit. I kept going over the whole Thornbloom horror in my mind. And something wasn't right. Don't you remember, Dicken? That night in my office after they had grilled you all day. You asked me if I had caught even a glimpse of Thornbloom in the library."

"And you hadn't."

"No, because of the stacks. But Dicken, you couldn't have known anything about the library. That was held in the strictest confidence. Only a few campus security people and the Secret Service knew about it. Nobody else, not even Laurencia. The only way you could have known about it, is if you had been there."

"I see. How clever. How very clever of you, Congresswoman. I underestimated you. Everyone is always underestimating you."

The others had arrived now, and she could feel them standing behind her.

And though she could not see, she could feel the guns pointed directly at Dicken Proctor, who said quietly:

"And I suppose you have figured out how I—well, how the voice told me to manage the other thing."

"Yes. It was coffee. The coffee you always loved to make. The two thermoses of coffee you gave to Thornbloom on the morning of that fatal flight. One for him, one for the pilot. So that they would be sure to drink enough of whatever you put in it."

"It wasn't much. Just…something to make them both sleep. Whenever the crash happened, I'm sure they were unaware of it. No pain. I owed old Thornbloom that much, even though he had allowed himself to become an instrument of evil."

"And the body we found…"

"A nobody. A nothing. Possessed of only one quality that killed him, but that also made him useful to me."

"He looked like Thornbloom."

"Yes, remarkably so. I remember being almost thunderstruck by it as I saw him, through the window of that hovel, stumbling out of whatever bar he had come from and going toward the alley he would sleep in. I befriended him, offered him a dry place to sleep…"

"And gave him an overdose of heroin."

"Yes. It all worked well. And, you must admit, it gave all of you such a sense of relief."

"Too much of a sense of relief. We let our guard down, just like you must have wanted us to."

"But it won't work now, will it? Those people behind you—they don't hear the voice."

"No, Dicken, they don't."

"Mister," Moon was saying, "Move away from that window!"

"Oh, I can't do that!"

"Move away!"

He looked at Nina and smiled:

"The voice wouldn't allow me to do that!"

"If you touch that rifle, Dicken, they'll kill you."

"I know. I know. But if I don't, the voice will not allow me to live. And so…do you know the Auden poem? *Musée des Beaux Arts?* All the people…"

He gestured out toward the stadium, where the crowd was cheering madly and Laurencia was mounting the platform.

"…all the people going about their business, not noticing that a little boy had fallen out of the sky.."

So saying, he lurched forward.

He was halfway out the window when Sylvia, as quick as she had been when she dove on Nina and saved her life, reached him, wrapped her strong arms around his upper legs, and pulled him back in

So that only the rifle fell out of the window.

And so that, just as Laurencia Dalrymple was proudly announcing:

"Sisters and Brothers, we did it! Two of the three women candidates running in referenda today WON THEIR RACES!"

Jubilation in the crowd.

"And tonight, NO STRIKE! Go home to your husbands, women! And, as you have learned from Helen Reddington's magnificent rendering of Lysistrata—let the tips of your shoes point toward the ceiling, wiggle all you want—and even assume the position of the hungry lion! Just remember—women are coming to power—and the power of war is going away!"

So that, just as she was saying these things, the rifle was clattering harmlessly on the top of a closed garbage bin below.

CHAPTER TWENTY: THE NEW VOICE IN CONGRESS

And now it was July 5.

The *Lysistrata* festival was over.

And Bay St. Lucy could resume its normal life.

A life which centered around the town hall.

Where Nina now found herself, surrounded by a group that included Jackson Bennett, Edie Towler, and Paul and Macy Cox.

But it was to her, Nina, that Jackson was now speaking:

"Nina, two things I guess I need to tell you."

"All right. Shoot."

"The first concerns Dicken Proctor."

"Poor man."

"Dangerous man. But he's in Jackson now, at a mental facility. He just sits and stares at the wall. What will happen to him...well, no one is sure. But the whole story is being kept strictly hush-hush. No one needs the sensationalism at this point."

"No."

"And the second is, we heard from the governor."

"And?"

"And he goes along with it, but with regrets. He accepts your resignation from the House of Representatives."

"That's a relief."

"Nina, are you sure that we can't..."

She shook her head:

"It was a glorious adventure, Jackson. I'll never forget it. Not one minute of it. And I thank all of you so much for making it possible. But I belong here. I knew that the second I stepped off the plane two days ago."

"All right then."

"But what about the other request?"

"He's amenable. Mainly because of all you've done. But the expense of another special election…no, he thinks he's got the backing to appoint the successor you suggested."

"Thank God."

She then looked at Paul.

"The Coxes," she said quietly, "are going to Washington after all."

Paul smiled:

"I hope you won't regret your decision, Nina."

"I know I won't. I think what we're looking at here is a long and prosperous political career. And I know you're going to make us all proud. And I know you're going to make the state of Mississippi proud. And all I can say is that I am proud to know you, and congratulate you…"

Then she smiled and said:

"Congratulations, Congresswoman Macy Cox!"

EPILOGUE

The following morning at ten o'clock she Vespa'd home from a few hours of puttering at Elementals, to find Jackson Bennett's car parked in her driveway.

She parked the Vespa, got off it, and walked to the foot of her stairway.

Jackson was coming out of the house.

"Did you bring him home, Jackson?"

"Sure did. The girls are going to miss him though."

"Thanks for taking care of him."

"Sure. Hey, I did have one question about this nut Proctor, or whatever his name was."

"Ask it?"

"How did he smuggle a deer rifle into Bay St. Lucy."

"Everybody thought it was a golf bag. He was known to be a golf nut. On a commercial flight he would have been checked and caught, but this was just the Senator's private plane. No one thought to look.

"I see. Well, I guess it's all clear now. I'm going to take off. And thanks for everything Nina. The country is different now. We don't know what will happen in November, but..."

"The Lissies will happen, Paul. And they'll keep happening."

"I hope that's true, Nina. I really do."

"Good bye, Jackson."

"Bye for now."

He got into his car, started it, and drove away.

She climbed the stairs and opened the door.

A small furry animal approached her, rubbed back and forth against her ankle, looked up at her, and said:
"Arrrrrgggh."
Which in cat means:
"Where the Hell have *you* been?"

THE END

ABOUT THE AUTHORS

Pam Britton (T'Gracie) Reese is an Assistant Professor in the Communication Science and Disorders Department at Indiana/Purdue University at Fort Wayne. Previously, she worked as a speech pathologist in schools in private practice. She was also a supervisor in communication disorders at Ohio University. She likes nothing better, professionally, than helping small, silent two-year-old boys start talking. She has also published books about autism with LinguiSystems for the last 15 years. *The Circle of Autism* was previously published online at *ken*again e-magazine*.

Joe Reese is a novelist, playwright, storyteller, and college teacher. He has published four novels, several plays, and a number of stories and articles. When he's not teaching (English and German), he enjoys visiting elementary schools, where he tells stories from his Katie Dee novels and talks to students about writing. He and his wife Pam have three children: Kate, Matthew, and Sam.